Dulecia D King has always wanted to write, but lived a very busy life and never found the time to be able to fully concentrate. Retired, living on her boat and being one of the vulnerable people, not allowed out during the 2020 Covid-19 lockdown, has knuckled her down to fulfilling her life's ambitions. She hopes you enjoy reading *I Feel Safe in the Church* as much as she did writing it.

To

Michael
and Denise
a wonderful couple

Sincerely

Dulecia D King

xx

Dulecia D King

I FEEL SAFE IN THE CHURCH

AUSTIN MACAULEY PUBLISHERS™

LONDON • CAMBRIDGE • NEW YORK • SHARJAH

A CIP catalogue record for this title is available from the British Library.

ISBN 9781398439108 (Paperback)
ISBN 9781398439115 (Hardback)
ISBN 9781398439122 (ePub e-book)

www.austinmacauley.com

First Published 2022
Austin Macauley Publishers Ltd®
1 Canada Square
Canary Wharf
London
E14 5AA

I would like to thank the staff of Austin Macauley Publishers for their help in production of this book.

Enjoying a beautiful walk out in the countryside in Norfolk on a sunny spring day, just coming to a church, I thought I would go into the grounds and have a look around the grave stones. I find them so interesting to read, and I visualise how things must have been in their day. Some are so old and have been left for years and forgotten about and ones that could be made out were so young. There were new ones with fresh flowers on and made now to last longer. I sat down for a while and pored a mug of tea from my flask and lit a cigarette and looked around the grounds so peaceful; no sound from anywhere just birds singing, and a little breeze blowing through the trees. Something made me turn and look at the church. I felt someone was behind me, but no one was there. I put my cup and flask away and put my cigarette out in my little mobile ashtray and took a walk over to the church entrance, thinking there may be a service going on. But no, the door was closed and everywhere was quiet. Then, just as I turned to head away, I heard crying! There was no one. I could see outside so I walked up to the door and tried the handle. It was very stiff but it then turned and opened. It was very cold inside with the concrete floors and very dark, but I could just see from the light coming through the stained glass. I called out, was anyone there, but no answer. I thought I must be imagining things so went back outside and closed the stiff door behind me. Time was getting on so I made my way back home. That night, I went to bed early but I couldn't get that crying sound out of my head and I felt that I didn't do enough to investigate it. That night, I had a very disturbing dream but when I woke up, I couldn't remember what it was that happened; only that it was about the church that I had visited. I kept saying to myself, don't be stupid I'm just imagine things, but I couldn't stop thinking about it.

In the end, I said to myself, that's it, I'm going back there just to get some peace of mind. It was very windy that day, but I was determined to go back and have another look inside the church. As I walked into the churchyard, the wind was howling through the tree. It made it feel very eerie and spooky, but I braved up and went to the church door. It was very stiff, and as I opened it, the wind blew through, giving such a gust that I quickly turned around and shut the door behind me, making it very dark inside. I slowly walked down the aisle looking along each row of seats as I went along softly calling out, "Is anybody there?" I then reached the altar but there was nothing I could see anywhere, so I sat down to take in the tranquillity of the church and imagining what it was like on Sunday service and at weddings and being full of people. *What was that!*

I heard something but couldn't make out what it was or who.

There it is again!

"Who's there?" I called out, then I heard a sobbing. It sounded like a child,

"Please come out whoever you are and talk."

Then this little figure appeared, all bedraggled, long uncombed dark hair, clothes all crumpled and dirty; a little girl of about ten years old.

"Hello, there."

The little girl did not answer. She just sobbed and sobbed then she quietly said a few words I could hardly make out because of her sobbing.

"Come and sit here with me, sweetheart, and talk to me. What the matter is?"

She slowly moved up to me and sat down. The sweet little thing was really in need of a good bath, but even so I put my arm around her to comfort her.

"What is your name, sweetheart?"

In her tearful little voice, she answered, "Annie."

"Were you here yesterday, Annie?"

"Yes."

"Have you been here all night?"

"I've been here all week. I've got nowhere to go, and I feel safe here."

"All week? My word! You poor little thing. Have you had anything to eat?"

"I've got biscuits and there is plenty of water here to drink."

"But where are your parents?"

"My mum is buried here, and my dad don't want me."

"Oh! That's awful my dear. Is that why you are here to be near your mum?"

"Yes, but I can't find her grave. I've look at everyone and her grave is not there."

"Look, my dear, I don't live far away. Would you like to come back with me and get warm and have something to eat and drink?"

"Yes, I would but I mustn't be seen by anyone because I will get put away."

"I will make sure that doesn't happen to you. Plus, it's started to get dark now so it will make it easier not to be seen. Come on then, let's get you in the warm."

We walked along the quiet countryside and didn't see anyone. My cottage was on its own in the country and my nearest neighbours were half a mile away, which was the farm house. Soon as we got home, I put the kettle on and sat Annie in front of the fire, as I didn't know how long since Annie had eaten and all she had was biscuits. It wouldn't be wise to make her a full-on meal as it would upset her, so I thought homemade soup and bread would be good for her and easy on her tummy.

"Annie, I'm going to make some soup. Would you like some?"

"I will try, but I've got used to not eating, so I don't know if I can get it down me, but thank you." Annie sat dazing into the fire, and I gave her a nice warm cup of tea while I carried on making the soup and prepared the table in the kitchen.

"Annie, would you like to come through to the kitchen? The tea is ready now."

"This smells nice, miss … Sorry I don't know your name."

"It's Dee. Yes I made this myself; not out of a tin. I like to cook up and liquidize leftover food and make into soups. They don't always turn out nice," I said laughingly.

Annie sat there eating her bread and dipping it into the soup with her little cold grubby hands. I didn't have the heart to tell her to go and wash them in the situation.

"Oh! That was lovely, thank you."

"I'd like to offer you more, but we better take it steady for now so as not to upset your tummy. Perhaps you could have something else later?"

"But I have to get back to the church."

"Oh surely not, my dear. Wouldn't you like a nice comfortable bed to sleep in?"

"Really?"

"Yes, of course. I couldn't let you go back to there in the cold and dark, and I have a spare room which you could use."

"Thank you so much, Dee. Would you mind if I had a small bath. I am so dirty, and I wouldn't like to make your bed dirty also."

"I was already going to ask if you'd like to have a nice warm bath and give me your dirty clothes and I will have them washed and dry again for the morning."

"You're so kind, Dee, just like my mum was."

"When did your mum pass away, Annie?"

"Six months ago, but it seems like a lifetime ago."

"What did she die off?"

"A broken heart, I think. Dad was always shouting at her, and he was so mean to her. I could always hear her crying at night from my bedroom."

"That is sad, Annie. Anyway, we can talk lots more tomorrow after you have had a good night rest."

"Yes, I am feeling very tired now."

I got a dressing gown for Annie so she could change out of her dirty clothes. She pulled some more bits out of her bag.

11

A cross dropped on the floor, and she quietly picked it up. I could see a photo of a lady she had in her bag.

"Is that your mum, Annie?"

"Yes, and this is her cross; all that I have left of her. But the cross is broken, so I can't wear it."

"We will have to get that mended then, won't we? Let me have a look at it tonight and see if I can fix it."

"Thank you, Dee, you're so kind."

Annie had a long time in the bath, so I gave her a shout in case she had fallen asleep. But she hadn't, and I could hear her splashing about in there.

I shouted to her if she needed any help washing her hair, but she had already done it. Annie came back into the lounge after her bath in her dressing gown that I gave her, looking so very clean and what a pretty girl she was!

"Would you like me to dry your hair for you, Annie?"

"Yes, please."

"Come and sit down here by the fire, and I will get my hairdryer."

As I was drying her hair, she started to nod off.

"Come on, Annie, let's get you into bed. You're so tired."

She got up without any hesitation and wandered into her bedroom. Her eyes were closed as soon as her head touched the pillow. I tucked her up and turned down the light so she could still see if she got up in the night.

I put all of Annie's clothes in the washing machine and then sat down to look at her cross. It was just a link that had come undone, so I re-chained it and laid it on her pillow beside her, while she was still sound asleep, bless her!

I finished washing Annie's clothes and then put them into the dryer which does a cycle through the night on cheap electricity tariff and then had a shower and got myself off to bed.

That night, I couldn't sleep very well thinking about Annie and how I could help her. Surely someone was out looking for her, and what about her school? Oh no! I do believe the children are on school holidays, but what about her dad? What an evil man. How could people be like that exist, and she is such a sweet innocent child. All these things were going through my head, but one thing was for sure, being retired and widowed with children grown up, I had lots of time on my hands, and I was sure going to help her live the life a little girl like that should live; happy and full of joy.

"Good morning, Annie. Did you sleep well?"

"Oh yes, it was so comfortable sleeping in a real bed; so warm and cosy. I didn't want to get up."

"You have a bed at home though, don't you?"

"No, I slept on the old broken down settee, that's if dad wasn't drunk and fell asleep on it first. Then I slept on the floor."

"That is really awful, Annie. Was your family really broke then?"

"It was alright when mum was alive, but she did go out to work also, and there was always food on the table. I always had nice clean clothes to wear, but when mum died and dad started drinking heavy, everything went bad. So yes, I think we were broke. Dad was selling everything he could to make money, but he was spending it on alcohol and got drunk every night. I got free school meals, so I was surviving. I soon learned how to do my own washing and ironing and I tried to keep the place clean."

"What about family? Do you have any relatives?"

"I don't know. I've never seen anyone, and mum and dad never spoke of anyone."

"So what happened when you left home a week ago? You said your dad didn't want you."

"He said some awful things to me when I got home from school. He had been drinking and he was swaying about. I asked him if he was alright, which was the wrong thing to have said."

"Am I alright? You stupid silly little animal, no of course I'm not alright. I have you to look after you, and you are nothing but a thorn in my side. I wish you died with your mother, you horrible child."

"That was a terrible thing to have said to a child. You must have felt really unwanted."

"Yes. More than that I was frightened, and I knew he didn't want me, so I took what little I had and left. You know the rest."

"Well, let's have some breakfast, to help us get a good start for the day. Then we can see how we can help you, Annie."

"Thank you for being so kind, Dee."

We had a nice full breakfast but all the time things kept going through my head; what can I do to help this child? I didn't want to go to the authorities for fear they would put her away. Then I thought, what if I went to see her father and tried to reason with him and she could stay here with me. She would be such a good company for me and I could help her live a normal life that a child should live.

"Annie, what would you think about me going t/
father and try talking to him about you staying witl

Annie started shaking and crying.

"You would do that for me? But you hardly know me,
Dee. I'm not your problem."

"Well, I've made it my problem, Annie. I think you are a
wonderful child who needs help, and I can give you that help
if you let me."

"But can I stay here when you go to see him? I'm too
frightened to go back there."

"Yes, of course you can. I would have preferred it that
way anyway."

Annie gave me her father's name and address; also her
mum's name. It wasn't far away; just down in the village. It
looked a rough area in a small crescent with about a dozen
semi-detached houses with cars everywhere. It looked more
like a breaker's yard. Number 24 was the first house in the
crescent; very shabby and in need of a good paint. As I walked
up to the door, I could see the curtains hanging off of the
pelmets, the windows were so dirty you couldn't see through
them. Anyway, I knocked on the door which came ajar as I
did. I waited a while but nobody came, so I gently pushed the
door open a bit more and called out, was anybody home. Still
no answer so I went slowly into the house. I'd never seen such
a mess in all my life washing up everywhere scraps of food
grease beer bottles rubbish bags, it was a mess.

"What do you think you're doing in my house?"

"Oh, I'm sorry! You made me jump. I did knock but
couldn't get an answer."

"And the reason being, miss, I didn't want to talk to you."

"Are you Mr Long?"

"None of your business."

"Please, I've come to talk to you about your daughter, Annie."

"I haven't got a daughter. Now clear off."

"Please, I know you are Mr Long and you do have a daughter called Annie, and if you won't talk to me then you will have to talk to the police."

"Why? What's she been up to?"

"She hasn't been up to anything. I found her up at St Mary's church where she had been hiding up for a week."

"So what's that got to do with me?"

"You are her father. Don't you care about her?"

"No I don't, so clear off."

"I will not clear off until I have had my say. You cannot bully me the same way you have her, Mr Long."

"You do not know what you are talking about, lady."

"Oh yes I do, Mr long, and she is staying with me until you can prove you can be a father to her."

"I knew it! You're after the bloody money aren't you."

"I am not after money whatsoever; I like the child and I will provide for her and see that she has a happy upbringing."

"Do what you want as long as you don't come after me for anything."

"There is one thing I would like to ask you."

"I knew it."

"That is, when I found Annie at St Mary's she said that her mother was buried there, but we couldn't find her grave."

"No, I couldn't afford one."

"Then can you tell me the date she died?"

"No, I bloody can't. Mind your own business and get out."

"Don't you even want to know where your daughter is living?"

"No."

"Good day to you, Mr Long. I won't bother you again."

As I left the house, I heard the door slammed behind me. It sent a shiver down my spine. What a nasty horrible man! He was everything Annie said he was. As I got to the gateway, a small scruffy boy ran up to me.

"Is Annie there, miss?"

"No she isn't. Are you a friend of hers?"

"I was; we were best friends, but she ran off without me a week ago and I haven't seen her since. Is she alright, miss?"

"Yes she is fine, would you like to see her?"

"Oh yes please! Where is she?"

"She is staying with me. I live just up the road in the Red house cottage on Back Lane. I'm going back there now if you would like to come with me, but you must go and tell your parents where you are headed."

"That's ok, miss. There's no one home till late."

My word! How are kids being brought up these days, I thought.

"Come on then, let's go and surprise Annie. My name is Dee. What is your name?"

"Tommy."

"Well, Tommy, how long have you known Annie?"

"We started the same school together. Annie is a month older than me. We had to sit on the floor in the classroom and I started to cry and all the kids laughed at me except Annie. She put her arm around me and we've been friends ever since."

17

We arrived home and I called after Annie. There was no answer.

"Come on in, Tommy. She must be in the garden. You sit there and I will go and see."

"Annie," I called out for her as I walked down the garden, then I saw her. She was stroking a little dog.

"Hello, Dee, look who I found."

"Where did you find him?"

"He was scratching at the back door, and when I opened it he jumped up at me crying and wagging his tail. I gave him some water and a biscuit. Was that alright, Dee?"

"Yes, of course it was, but we will have to find out who he belongs to, as they will be worried about him."

"Can I look after him until we find them, please?"

"Yes, I do not see any reason why not, but I have got another surprise for you. Someone is waiting in the kitchen to see you."

"It's not my dad, is it?" Looking white as a ghost and shaking. "No, I have seen that man and he is everything you say he is." I opened the back door; Annie walked through.

"TOMMY!"

"ANNIE!"

They both hugged each other. It was so lovely to see them so happy together.

"Why don't you show Tommy around, Annie, while I get tea ready for all of us, that's if you can stay for tea, Tommy. What time will you have to be home?"

"Yes, thank you, Dee, I would love to stay. Mum and dad don't get back until the pubs shut." I could see how they both got on so well together. They both had parents that didn't care about them poor little things.

I got on with making supper still with so much going through my head. I must find out when they are going back to school and go and have a word with the head mistress. Oh! And I had better take a note to our village post office/ shop and put an ad in about the missing dog. It looks like my life is going to be pretty full from now on.

"Tea is ready, kids, come and eat."

We all sat down at the kitchen table and dug in to the food. I had made a cottage pie which I find always goes down well with most people.

"This is delicious, Dee."

"Yes it is really good. Dee is a good cook."

"Oh I wouldn't say that. I'm just a basic cook, and as long as you enjoyed it, that's the main thing."

"That reminds me, when do you kids start back to school?"

"Next Wednesday, Dee."

"I'd better come with you, Annie, and have a chat with your headmistress. Just to explain the situation and that you are staying here with me."

"Oh, lucky you, Annie, you staying here. Can I always come here to visit please?"

"Of course you can, Tommy, any time you like, as long as you tell your parents where you are. I don't want to be had up for hiding stowaway children, haha!"

"Yes I will, Dee, if I see them or I will leave a note for them. It was different before because Annie was always at my place, as I wasn't allowed at her house. Her dad was so mean. He found me in the garden once; he went bonkers. *GET OUT OF HERE NOW!* He shouted at me, so I ran off, never went there again. I reckon he had dead bodies buried there."

"You mustn't say things like that, Tommy. He is just a nasty man who doesn't like children."

"But I have heard grownups talking, Dee, and there have been people missing, and they say they don't trust him and that he was put away once in a prison but I think it was a mental home."

"Is that true, Annie?"

"He wasn't around for a while, and mum just said he had gone away to work. That's probably why none of the neighbours spoke to us."

"Well, let's forget about him now and be happy."

Woff woff.

"Oh yes, I forgot about you, little fella. We will have to find out who you belong to in the morning. When the post office opens, I shall put an advert in the window and see if anyone claims him, but now, Tommy, I had better walk you home."

"No, I'm alright on my own, Dee."

"Don't be silly! Besides, we can all go and take the dog for a walk at the same time."

Annie smiled with excitement, and went and found a rope that we could use as a lead while I cleared the table.

We all set off down the road, not forgetting the torch as it was beginning to get dark. Tommy and Annie went off running with the dog who was enjoying every minute of it. They all looked so happy, which in turn made me feel happy. Just then, I could see a light on in the distance. Tommy and Annie came running back.

"Dee, the post office shop is still open. Shall we go in?"

"Yes, go on then."

"Hello, Mrs Adams. I didn't realise you stayed open this late. I was going to come and see you in the morning to put a note in your window."

"Yes, Mrs King, since Mr Adams passed away, I stay open later now to see more people and keep me occupied. Are these your grandchildren, Mrs King?"

"No, Annie here is now staying with me, as she lost her mother not so long ago, and this is her friend Tommy who we are walking back home, and this little man here we think is lost, that's why I wanted to put a notice in your window."

Mrs Adams looked curiously at the children and then turned to the dog.

"Do you know, I do believe that is Miss Robertson dog. Yes I'm sure it is, and I think his name is Patch."

The dog seemed to have responded to that name.

"If you can tell me where she lives, then we could take him back to her."

"She is very old and probably will be in bed now. Besides, it's a really run down old place and hard to find at night. Leave it till the morning and I will pop round and see her before I open up the shop. Will you be alright having him for the night, Mrs King?"

"Yes, of course. Annie wanted to keep him if they couldn't find his owner."

"Come on then, kids, let get you home, Tommy, and we will come back here tomorrow; goodbye Mrs Adams."

"Yes, goodnight to you all. See you tomorrow."

As we got to the little estate where Tommy lived, we had to pass Annie's house. It was all in darkness. Annie was walking very close to me; hoping that she couldn't be seen.

"Don't worry, Annie, you're with me now."

We walked Tommy up to his front door; his house was also in darkness.

"Doesn't look like your parents are home yet, Tommy."
"No, they won't be home until the pub shuts."

"Will you be alright on your own?"

"Yes, I'm a big boy now," he said as he opened the front door and put the light on in the hall way.

"Can I come and visit tomorrow, Dee?"

"Yes, Tommy, of course you can; bye for now."

"Bye, Tommy."

Tommy was waiving as we walked away out of site.

"Annie, your dad told me he couldn't afford a head stone when your mother passed away, so that's why you couldn't find it."

Annie started to cry.

"So I won't have anything now of her existence. That's not fair."

"We will make an appointment to go and see the rector at St Mary's and talk to him about it. Can you remember the date she died?"

"It was last winter, I think. It was October but I can't remember what date."

"Don't worry about it. Now let's get home and have a nice cup of cocoa, watch TV for a while and then bed."

As we past Annie's dad's house again, we noticed a dim light on; looked like a candle burning at that stage. The dog pulled to a halt and growled.

"What's the matter with you, Patch? Don't you like that house either?" Annie asked him. I was getting a bit curious about Mr Long and this house and how he was acting and then the things Tommy said. Oh! I must be getting tired and letting my imagination get the better of me.

"Come, you two, let's get home."

That following morning, I awoke to a knocking on the front door. Who could it be this early?

"Why, Mrs Adams, you're early."

"Yes, I'm sorry to have woken you up so early, but I called round to Miss Robertson like I said I would, and you just won't believe what had happened."

"Please come in, Mrs Adams. You're shaking. I'll put the kettle on. Now sit down there and get your breath back."

"Thank you, Mrs King. Oh! It was horrible. I found poor Miss Robertson sitting in her old chair. I thought she was asleep and then her hand fell open and there was a note. Here, you should read it please. I can't get my breath."

WHO EVER FINDS ME, DO NOT WORRY. MY LIFE HAS COME TO AN END. I AM OLD AND HAVE HAD A GOOD LIFE. ESPECIALLY THE LAST FIVE YEARS WITH MY DEVOTED DOG, PATCH. I LET HIM LOOSE YESTERDAY AND TOLD HIM TO GO AND FIND A NICE KIND PERSON WHO WILL TAKE CARE OF YOU. I TRULY HOPE HE DID FIND SOMEONE AND THAT HE WILL BE HAPPY AS HE WAS HERE. I HAVE NO FAMILY BUT I HAVE LIVED A HAPPY LIFE BUT NOW IT'S TIME FOR ME TO GO AND MEET THAT GREAT MAN UP IN THE SKY. THANK YOU, ENID ROBERTSON.

"Oh wow, Mrs Adams, and you were the first person to see this? You poor thing! Here, put that down your neck and get your breath back. So, are the police there now?"

"No, she didn't have a telephone, so I came straight here."

"Don't worry. I will call them from here for you and explain everything to them." At that moment, Annie came downstairs, rubbing her eyes and yawning.

"What's up? Why is everyone up early? And, Mrs Adams, why are you here?"

"Sit down, Annie, and have a cup of tea. We have some unhappy news but also some good news."

"Where is Patch?"

"He is still asleep in my bed. I think it's too early for him to get up yet."

"Well, the thing is, we found or rather Mrs Adams found Patch's owner and, unfortunately, she was old and had passed away, but she had left a note as she dearly loved Patch and wanted someone loving to take care of him and make him happy as he had made her happy."

"Oh yes! I will make him happy, Dee, and love him so much. Can I keep him, please?"

"Yes, Annie, you can because he chose you. In Miss Robertson's letter she said she let Patch out and told him to go and find someone who will love him, and he came and found you, Annie."

"I will love him always. Thank you, miss Robertson, for sending him to me."

"Right then, can you help yourself to cereals and get Mrs Adams another cup of tea? I've got some phone calls to make."

I got on the phone to the police and told them what had happened and we arranged to meet them over at Miss Robertson's cottage that morning where a doctor would also be present. "Ok, Annie, I'm going to leave you in charge while Mrs Adams and myself go over to Miss Robertson's house to meet with the police and a doctor. Don't forget Tommy is coming this morning, and there is food on the side there for Patch, and I will be as quick as I can."

"Yes alright, Dee, we will be fine."

Mrs Adams and I went off to Miss Robertson's cottage. When we got there, the police were already there. We introduced ourselves to them and Mrs Adams told them she was the one who found her this morning and also handed over the note which she had clenched in her hand.

"I am DCI West, mam, we are just waiting on the arrival of Miss Robertson's GP doctor, Tindal. He shouldn't be too long now. Then we will know how the old lady died."

I hadn't realised Dr Tindal was still alive. He must be in his nineties now. If it's the same one, I do believe he bought me into the world. Just at that moment, a frail old weathered-looking chap came slowly walking up the pathway. *My word! It is the same Dr Tindal.*

"Good morning, ladies. I've come to see old Enid."

At that time, one of the policemen came to meet him and took him inside the cottage. We all followed.

"I came to see old Enid a couple of days ago. I thought the old girl would out live me but she had a bad ticker. I said I could send her into hospital but she was having none of it. Look, Bob, she said I'm too old to be mucked around with now. All I care about is my dog, Patch, and I am going to go home in my own surroundings with Patch and pass away with dignity. I've had a good life as you know, and now it's time for me to make room for someone else to come into this world. Yes, she was a wise old women and knew what she wanted."

"What about her family, Dr Tindal?"

"No, she had no family, but that was the way she wanted it. She said to me once, *I've seen so much tragedy in my life; broken marriages, unwanted babies, and I'm not going to live my life like that.*"

"So, what did she do with her life?"

"She was a nurse, and she loved her work and looking after other people. She had a heart of gold, and I know she was writing a book on her life. I don't know if she finished it, but I would love to have read it, I know that."

The policeman interrupted,

"So can you verify, Dr Tindal, that Miss Robertson died of a heart attack?"

"Yes, my dear boy, her heart stopped in the end."

"Thank you, sir, we will get the body taken away then."

"Yes, ok, and one thing I do know what she told me is that you will find all her wishes which she had written down in a folder in that bureau over there and the key is in the tea caddy in the kitchen."

DCI west came up to us looking rather concerned.

"Ladies, this is very difficult for me as at this point. I would be contacting the next of kin so that they can make all the appropriate arrangements, but as there isn't any I can contact. Would you ladies stay here while we go through Miss Robertson's papers?"

"I really need to go and open up the post office; it's pension day, and there will be a few old chaps in need of their money."

"You go on, Mrs Adams, I can wait here for a while with the policeman."

"Ok, I'm off then; will talk later."

DCI West found the key and opened up the bureau. Everything was neatly positioned and in its place, but there in front for anyone to see was the folder Dr Tindal had mentioned. DCI west opened the folder; inside was a note from Miss Robertson saying whoever is reading this then Dr Tindal has told you where to find it upon my death. Please contact Nelson hide and partners for the attention of Mr Hide. Everything is with them and will carry out my wishes. "Oh well, that makes it easier. I can now contact them and they can take over. Thank you for staying, Mrs King."

"That's quite alright. I'd better get off now you know where to contact me if you need to, don't you?"

"Yes, Mrs King. I have everything here."

"Well you sure turned out to be a lovely lady, Dee."

"Oh you made me jump, Dr Tindal. I didn't think you would remember me after all these years."

"I don't have to remember faces, my dear. I keep my own records of everyone I have delivered in my life. I know who's who and where they are and what they are doing."

"That's interesting, Dr Tindal. Perhaps we could have a chat sometime, if that's ok?"

"Yes, my dear, here's my number; give me a call. Now, I must go and get some rest myself. Good day to you, Dee."

"Bye, Dr Tindal."

When I arrived home, Tommy and Annie were playing in the garden with Patch.

"Hi, kids, I'm home."

Tommy and Annie came running up the path with Patch.

"Hi, Dee, how did it all go?"

"Oh, don't ask! It was so sad, but now I need you two to cheer me up, so come on, kids, what shall we do this afternoon?"

"Dee, can we go to St Mary's again? I want to show Tommy where you found me."

"Yes, of course we can, will give Patch a good walk also."

When we got to the church, the door was open; inside was a lady who looked as if she was praying.

"Shush, children, we don't want to disturb that lady. Let's have a walk around outside for a while."

"No, don't go. I was just leaving myself."

"Sorry, we didn't mean to disturb you."

"You didn't. I always come here once a week in the hope of one day finding my mother, but she must be so old now. I don't suppose she is still alive, which makes it worse as I would never have had the chance to meet her."

"I'm so sorry to hear that. Did she live around here?"

"I don't know, please forgive me. Sit down for a while. My name is Elizabeth."

"Mine is Dee, and this is my little adopted daughter, Annie, and her friend Tommy, and of course our dog, Patch."

"Please to meet you all. I don't see many people to chat to these days. Do you live near?"

"Yes, down in the village in red house cottage."

"Well that's a coincidence. I live at the Red house up on the hill."

"My word! That's a mansion. Our cottages used to be part of that estate."

"That's right. Many years ago though, my adopted parents sold off a lot of land around here."

"So have you always lived there?"

"No, I moved away to London when I got married and moved back a year ago when my adopted parents died in a car accident and they left the place to me. It wasn't till I came back and looked through all the papers, I found a letter from my real mother and it was addressed to me."

"How wonderful! What did it say? Or am I being too nosy?"

"Of course not. It's good to be able to talk about it. Here, I've got it with me. Please go ahead and read it. It will only make me cry again if I read it."

My darling daughter. I named you Elizabeth so I pray you still have the same name. Giving you up will be the worst thing in my life I will have to do. I was very young when I gave birth to you and unmarried. There was a war going on and I was in the forces as a nurse. I met a soldier who sadly was killed during the war, and then found I was pregnant with you, my darling. I had no money and wouldn't be able to provide for you.

The Browne's from the big Red house couldn't have children and wanted so much to adopt you, but the stipulation was that I had no contact with you and they would give you this letter when they thought it right to do so.

I agreed to this, my darling, as I knew you would never want for anything and you would have a good life, which I do sincerely hope you have, my love. When this war is over, I shall visit St Mary church every week and pray for you and perhaps, one day, we will bump into each other. Have a wonderful life, my darling.

Your mother
xxx

"Oh! how sad, Elizabeth. So is that all you have to go on that she came here every week to pray?"

"Afraid so, I don't even know her name, and this might not even be the same church. There are several St Mary's churches around. It's just this is the nearest one to the Red house, and she would have known that, so that's why I come here. But I'm in my 60s now so she could be 80 to 90 years old and could be dead, for all I know."

"Get down, Patch."

"I'm terribly sorry but he seems really taken to you."

"That's alright. I love dogs, and you're a beauty aren't you?"

"So have you any family of your own?"

"Not really. I lost my husband to a heart attack a few years ago, and my one and only child left home after a terrible argument years ago because she wanted to marry this awful man and he was awful. We knew more about him than she did, but she wouldn't hear a word against him and told us she never wanted to see us again and moved out. That was fifteen years ago, but she was twenty nine at the time and was old enough to do what she wanted. I couldn't stop her, so she is probably somewhere in London still. I tried to find her when her father died, but no luck."

"How horrible for you, Elizabeth. Please why don't you come and join us for dinner sometime. I won't take no for an answer now. Here is my number, so call me."

"Thank you, Dee, I will. It's nice to know I have a friend to talk to."

"Well, we must be off now as we need to try and catch the rector if he is still around."

"Ok, bye for now and see you all again soon."

The rector's name was Michael Heart and lived in the vicarage next to the church.

"Annie, can you and Tommy take Patch for a little walk around while I go and have a chat with the rector? I won't be long."

"Yes alright, Dee."

I knocked on the door of the vicarage. A very pleasant lady came to open the door. "Hello there, how can I help you?"

"Hello. I just wondered if the rector was available."

"He is in his office at the moment, but if you would like to come in and wait, I will go and see if he can see you. Who shall I say wants to see him?"

"Mrs Dee King."

A couple of minutes past, then the reverend appeared.

"Hello, Mrs King, I understand you would like to speak to me. Please come through to my office."

I followed through with him to his office; paperwork everywhere.

"I can see you're busy."

"Oh, don't take any notice of the mess, Mrs King, it's always like this, but I know where everything is. Please have a seat, and tell me how I can help, Mrs King."

"Please call me Dee. Well, I found a young girl sleeping in your church last week."

"Really?"

"Yes. She was very upset, she had lost her mother six months ago and she thought her mother was buried here. But she looked everywhere for her headstone but could not find it."

"Poor child! What is her name?"

"It's Annie, Annie Long, but according to her father, he couldn't afford a headstone."

"Do you know the exact date of her mother's death and her first name?"

"It's Susan long and Annie thinks it was about October last year, but unfortunately her father is impossible and said he couldn't remember."

"Well, let me see ... well definitely not anything here in October, but let's have a look through the other months ... no, I'm sorry to have to say, but I have nothing listed here at all for last year. Let me check if it was a cremation instead."

Well, Reverend's heart certainly did know his way through all his filing system even if it was a mess. He got up, went to his filing cabinet and pulled out more papers.

"I'm sorry, Dee, but there shows no record of a Susan long decease in any records."

"I don't know what to say, and what am I going to say to Annie?"

"I thinks it's best you talk with Annie's father again. It maybe that he's still in mourning and doesn't want to talk about it."

"Yes, you're right, reverend."

"Call me, Michael."

"Well thank you for your time, Michael."

"No problem, my dear; anytime."

Well now I didn't know what to do. So many things were going through my head; no record of Susan's death, could it be that Susan ran away, no she wouldn't leave Annie behind. What do I do now?

"Dee, we're over here, look at Patch, he keeps digging and won't stop."

"Patch! Over here, now."

Patch came running and wagging his tail and panting like mad.

"Good thing I remembered to bring water, wasn't it Patch."

"Look at all the mess you made. Good thing it wasn't someone's grave."

"Come on then, you two. It's getting late and you start back to school tomorrow."

"Shall I call for you on the way to school tomorrow, Tommy?"

"Why don't we all call for Tommy on the way. I'm going to see your headmistress also."

"Oh yes! That will be great. I can tell everyone you're my mum."

"More like your grandma, Annie. I'm a bit old to be your mum. Besides, they know your mum and what she looks like."

"No they don't, Dee. She never came to the school with me, and I could never have anyone round as Tommy told you what happened when he tried."

Things were getting more and more mysterious now. Perhaps Annie's headmistress will be able to shed some light when I speak to her. We walked Tommy home.

"Bye, Tommy. See you tomorrow."

"Bye, Annie. Bye, Dee."

As we passed Annie's old house, Patch again stood rigid and growled.

"Come on, Patch."

"Why trying to pull him away?"

"I wonder why he does that every time we go past my old house."

"I don't know."

We got home. Annie went up to her room and Patch followed her. She had made her room so nice and cosy. I gave her a small TV which she could have in there and a cosy old armchair which I had for years, but now I think Patch has claimed that for himself. Annie had put a few pictures on the walls of her favourite rock stars, but one thing I did notice, apart from her little locket, she had no photos on show of her mum.

"Do you have any photos of your mum, Annie? Which you could put in a frame on your side table?"

"No, Dee, I don't think we even had a Camera, that's why that locket is so precious to me. It's the only picture I have of my mother."

"What about you, Annie? Do you not have any pictures of you?"

"I have the photos which were taken at school every year."

"Your parents must have had wedding photos of when they got married."

"Never seen any, Dee."

"Oh well, I will go and get some tea ready for us, yes and you too, Patch."

I went and lit the fire in the lounge as it was getting a bit chilly, then went into the kitchen to make tea, and saw that Annie had ironed her school clothes and put them neatly on the boiler to air. You could tell that she had been used to looking after herself, poor thing.

The next day, I walked with Annie to school. As promised, we called on Tommy not before Patch having his usual growling as we went past Annie's old house. When we arrived at the school, Annie and Tommy went off to the playground and I went into the secretary office to see if I could speak to the headmistress.

"Hello, Mrs King. I am Miss Wilden, the headmistress. I understand you wish to have a chat with me."

"Yes, Miss Wilden, it's about one of your pupils here, Annie Long."

"Yes please come through to my office and take a seat, Mrs King. Now, how can I help you?"

"Well, it started over a week ago now. I was out walking and went to St Mary's church where I found young Annie hiding in there and found out she had been sleeping in there for the past week."

"Really?"

"Yes, and once more I went to see her father as her mother had passed away and he told me to clear off and mind my own business and he couldn't have cared less about Annie."

"No!"

"So now Annie is living with me, and I am looking after her."

"Well that's very kind of you, Mrs King, but have you informed the police?"

"No. Annie is so frightened of being put away."

"That's all very well, Mrs King, but they have to be informed about all this."

"But she is so happy now. She has a proper home, she has her friend, Tommy, and even has her own dog, Patch."

"That as it may be, Mrs King, but I have a duty of care to my pupils here, and I don't know you from Adam. Although you maybe a perfectly normal person, I don't know that, and I have to, in this situation, report it to my superiors; things have to be investigated."

"Well, you won't get anything out of Mr Long except abuse."

"Yes, but we have to investigate these things and you say Mrs Long has passed away. We don't know anything about this."

"You don't?"

"No, nothing has been passed on to us, and the social services would have intervened when there is a death in the family to make sure children are ok and being looked after alright and also inquire with the school. But there has been none of this. So yes, I am very concerned and worried myself Mrs King."

"When you put it like that, I can fully understand, Miss Wilden, and I also am more worried about it. All I could think of was making the girl happy as her father was so horrible, now I don't know what to do."

"Look, sit there, I will get some tea brought in while I go and make a few phone calls."

From the office, I could see all the children playing in the playground, and then the bell sounded and they all lined up and went to their classrooms. Then it all went quiet. At that moment, the secretary came through with a pot of tea on a tray and put it down on the desk. "Hello, Mrs King. I'm Mrs Willis, the school secretary. Miss Wilden won't keep you longer than necessary. She is just making some calls, please help yourself to tea."

"Thank you very much. That is kind of you."

Miss Wilden walked back into the office and sat down looking very concerned and wrote down a few things on a notepad and looked up at me and smiled.

"Well, Mrs King, I have spoken to social service. A lady there called Mary Baxter. She also is very concerned as she also has not heard about the death of Mrs Long and would like to come and see you this afternoon if that's alright with you. I've given her your details which you gave to me earlier and your phone number so she will call you first."

"Yes, that will be fine. Let's hope we can get this all sorted out soon so that Annie can start living a normal life."

"From what I can see, Mrs King, Annie is lucky to have found you."

"Thank you, Miss Wilden for all your help. I dare say we will be seeing more of each other now, so many thanks and goodbye to you."

"Goodbye, Mrs King."

'Phone rings…'

"Hello."

"Hello can I speak to Mrs Dee King, please?"

"This is Dee speaking."

"My name is Val Smith. I work for the local social service here in burgh St. Paul and Miss Wilden gave me your details to get in touch with you as you have young Annie Long staying with you after she had run away from home."

"Yes, that's right. But it wasn't the fact that she run away, more like her father pushed her away."

"Mrs King, would it be alright if I came and had a chat with you this afternoon?"

"Yes, any time after p.m."

"Shall we say p.m.?"

"Yes that would be fine."

Knock, knock, on the door.

"Mrs King? Val Smith. We spoke on the phone this morning."

"Yes, do come in."

"Thank you, what a lovely little cottage you have here."

"That's kind of you to say so. Please sit down and make yourself comfortable."

"Thank you, Mrs King."

"Please call me, Dee."

"Yes and I'm Val. Now I just want to take a short statement from you, about how you found Annie and when that was etc."

I explained everything to Val what happened the day that I found her and that I had been to see her father and how nasty he was and didn't even want to know where she was, and how frightened she was of him and also didn't want to get put away.

"So, Dee, didn't you think to phone the police?"

"No, not really. I thought if I could look after her and make her happy, as her father didn't want her and her mother had passed away, I would be helping the child."

"Yes, that is another problem. We cannot find any record of Mrs Long's death. So you see, we will have to inform the police to make some inquiries about it."

"Oh no, do you think something bad has happened to her?"

"I can't comment at this stage, Dee, but I will have to have a little chat with Annie also."

"She will be home from school shortly. Would you like to talk to her then?"

"Yes, sooner the better, Dee; the sooner we can get this all sorted out, the better for Annie."

I went out into the kitchen to make some tea. The back door opened. Patch came running through to meet Annie.

"Hello, Patch, have you missed me?"

"Annie, there is someone here to see you in the lounge."

"Who's that, Dee? It's not my dad, is it?"

"No, it's a lady from social services."

"She hasn't come to take me away. Please don't let her take me away, Dee."

"No, my dear, but she needs to know everything that's happened so she can sort something out about you staying here with me."

We went into the lounge and made ourselves comfortable by the fire, oh and Patch too; we can never leave him out now.

"Hello, Annie, my name is Val, Val Smith. He's a lovely doggie. Is he yours?"

"Yes, I think so, isn't he, Dee?"

"Yes, you see, Patch here came and found Annie here in the garden one day, and when we made inquiries, we found out that his owner was an old lady here who had passed away, and there was no one else to look after him."

"Well, that was lucky, Annie, that he found you."

"Annie, I can see you are happy here with Dee, but we have got no record of what happened to your mother, so I just need you to answer some questions for me, is that alright with you?"

"Yes."

"Now just tell me in your own words what happened the day your mother passed away."

"It was horrible. I came home from school and mum wasn't there. Dad was sitting in the lounge drinking as usual. I asked him where mum was, and he just shouted at me SHE IS DEAD. I cried out but I got no response from my dad. I asked him when she will be buried. He just said in a couple of weeks."

"Was she ill, Annie?"

"Not that I knew of."

"What was your life like at home before your mother passed away?"

"Mum was kind and looked after me. Although we didn't have much money and dad was always out drinking, which I didn't mind because we were happy when he was out."

"Did you have any friends, Annie?"

"I've always had one friend; Tommy."

"Yes, he still comes here to see Annie. They get on so well together."

"Did he come to see you at your home when your mother was alive?"

"Oh no, no one was allowed in the house, but Tommy came in one day looking for me, and my dad caught him; he went berserk."

"So do you have any relatives that come to see you?"

"No, no one, and mum never spoke of anyone."

"When your mother passed away, Annie, did your father get in touch with your school to tell them?"

"I don't know. I wasn't allowed to ask questions. I just had to get on with things on my own."

"Tommy was the only one I could talk to."

"Alright, Annie, that will be all for now. Enjoy the rest of your day, and I will call again and see you."

"Ok. Bye, Val."

I walked Val to the front door.

"Poor child, the things you get to hear in this job is unbelievable, Dee."

"Yes I can imagine. What happens now, Val?"

"Next, pay Mr Long a visit."

"Good luck with that."

"Yes, one visit I'm not looking forward to. Anyway, Dee, you have my number. Please don't hesitate to call me at any time, and I will call and see you again soon, bye for now."

"Bye, Val."

A few days went by and I received a letter in the post. It was from Mrs Robertson's solicitors, asking me to call them and make an appointment to see them, regarding the death of Miss Enid Robertson.

What on earth would they want to talk to me about? Feeling very curious, I called them straight away and made an appointment for the following day.

"Thank you for coming to see me so quickly, Mrs King. I'm Mr Eric Hide, Miss Enid Robertson was my client. Now I understand that you have Patch Enid's dog?"

"Oh no! Don't say someone has turned up to claim him."

"No, Mrs King. On the contrary, Enid would like you to keep him and she will pay you also for taking care of him."

"No, I don't want payment, I am looking after a little girl who lost her mother and Patch came and found her in my garden and now they are inseparable."

"That's a wonderful story, Mrs King, and I am so glad to hear it because Enid loved that dog so much. It was all she had, and she said to me before she died that she was sending Patch out to look for a new owner and that she told Patch that it must be someone who loves him as much as she. Well, I thought she was going a bit senile, but after hearing your story, I can see that's what she did, and he has done what she told him to do, how strange! Well anyway, she also asked me to vet the person who he goes to, which I have already done and I must say, Mrs King, you come up smelling of roses."

"Why on earth have you done all that for? Isn't that invasion of my privacy or something?"

"Sorry, it seems like that Mrs King but the thing is Enid had no family and she knew Patch would find the right person to go to, so she has left her whole estate to Patch with you as the beneficiary and asks that you do something worthwhile with the place and leave it in the memory of Patch when he does finally pass on."

"I'm lost for words, Mr Hide. I don't know what to say."

"Yes, there is a lot to take in at once, Mrs King, but you just think about it and I will get these papers drafted and sent over to you, so good day to you, Mrs King."

"Yes, good day."

I just did not know what I was doing. My mind was all over the place. I couldn't think straight, so I went for a walk to try and clear my head.

When I got home, Patch was jumping around wagging his tail.

"Come on then, Patch, let's go for a walk and meet Annie."

"Hi, Annie, thought we'd come and meet you."

"Deeeeee!"

"Shall we go to the little tea shop and have an ice cream?"

"Yes please. Can Tommy come also?"

"Yes, where is he?"

"Oh, he was naughty so got detention but he shouldn't be long now."

"What did he do wrong?"

"A silly boy was calling us names so Tommy hit him."

"Why was he calling you names?"

"Just because we always hang around together, kids think we're weird."

"That's not nice, but he really shouldn't go round hitting anyone."

"He calls me his knight in shining armour, hehe."

"Here he comes. Tommy would you like to come with us to the tea shop for ice cream?"

"Yes, please."

We got to the tea shop, found a table and ordered two ice creams and a coffee for myself. Just at that moment, Elizabeth came in; the lady we met at the church last week.

"Elizabeth! It's Dee, come and join us."

"Hello there, fancy bumping into you again so soon."

"I've just ordered coffee, would you like a cup?"

"Yes, please."

The waitress came along with our coffee and ice creams and we sat there; all having a nice social chat. I told everyone

43

about my visit with the solicitor and that we were now left with Enid's little cottage and grounds. Annie was so excited about it.

"We could turn it into a small animal park, Dee."

"That's not a bad idea, Annie, but there's a lot we need to know about animals, perhaps we should go and see a vet and get their views on it."

"Well, Dee, I might be able to help you out there. You see, I was a vet when we lived in London, but after my husband passed away, I decided to give it up. So any help you may need, I will be only too happy to give you a hand."

"That's marvellous, Elizabeth, thank you."

"So why don't we make a weekend of it and all meet up and go to Enid's cottage this weekend and see what we can do there?"

"Yes, I'm free this weekend, count me in."

"Can I come, please?"

"Yes, of course you can, Tommy, we wouldn't leave you out."

Everyone was so excited about the weekend, and things were starting to come together. Even Elizabeth seemed more happier, and what luck that she was a vet. I could see we were all going to get on well, even Patch was taken to Elizabeth. We all left the tea room and walked home together, dropping Tommy off at his house first.

"Bye, Tommy."

"Bye, Annie, see you tomorrow."

"Oh no! Patch don't start that again, come on. Do you know, Elizabeth, that is where Annie used to live. Her father still lives there, but every time we pass the house, Patch acts up like this, growling and snarling. I don't know what he would do if he wasn't on a lead."

"He obviously doesn't like the man, Dee."

"But he doesn't know him; at least I don't think so."

"Dogs have such a sense of understanding of people. They know straight away what sort of person you are whether you good or bad kind or unkind; he must have seen Annie's dad at some time and didn't like him and has never forgotten. Their sense of smell is so strong that he can smell him when you go by the house, and he must have remembered Annie, that's why he went to find her."

"Right this is where I turn off. See you guys tomorrow."

"Yes. Bye, Liz, will phone you first thing."

Annie, Patch, and myself carried on the walk to our house. Annie was so much part of my family now. I don't think I could do without her now. She has really brought a sparkle to my life, I know that. Seeing her and Patch skipping down the road and playing seems like she has been with me always.

"Have you got any homework to do, Annie?"

"Yes, just a little bit, and I've also got to write a short essay."

"Well if there is anything I can help you with, just ask."

"Thank you, Dee."

The evenings were getting nice and lighter now, so after tea we all went for a walk and I took my camera with me to take some nice pictures of Annie and Patch. I could see the big red house up on the hill and wondered what Elizabeth was doing all alone in that big house. I saw horses up on the grounds trotting around and wondered if Elizabeth rode, guess she probably did as she was a vet. It was a nice thought to think that we could all be friends and doing stuff together.

'Ring, Ring'

"Hello, Mrs King, this is Val Smith from the social services again."

"Yes, Hello there."

"Well, you were right about Mr Long. He was very argumentative and slammed the front door on me."

"Well, yes that doesn't surprise me for one minute; just the same with me."

"I have no alternative now but to inform the police, and I just thought I would put you in the picture first before I do as they will most probably want to talk to you and Annie also."

"Things aren't looking good at all, are they, Val? Do you think Annie's mother could still be alive?"

"I wouldn't like to comment at this stage, Dee, but yes things do not seem right."

While walking to school with Annie to pick up Tommy, also, Annie called out.

"Dee, look there is a police car outside my dad's house."

With that, Patch pulled so hard and slipped his lead and ran straight into the garden of Annie's old house. We heard Annie's dad shouting out at him.

"Oh, Dee, I'm too frightened to go in and get him."

"You stay there. I will get him."

"Clear off you dirty stinking animal."

With that he threw a big piece of wood at Patch.

"Leave that dog alone. He is mine!"

"Then you should keep him on a leash, shouldn't you?"

"I'm sorry his leash broke, it won't happen again."

As I walked up to Patch, I could see he had been digging again. This time, he had something in his mouth and ran quickly back to Annie before I could catch him. It was a good job the police were still in the house, as for some reason, I didn't think I would have gotten away so easily if they weren't.

"What has he got in his mouth, Annie?"

"Come here, Patch, let me have a look at what you have there. It's one of my mum's hair ribbons. This was her favourite one. She always wore this one because I bought it for her."

At that moment, Tommy came running up to us, "What are the police doing outside your house, Annie?"

"That's not my house anymore, and I don't care. I hope they take him away."

"Come on, you two, let's get off to school or you will be late. Do you want me to take your mum's ribbon and put it safely in your bedroom, Annie?"

"Yes, please, Dee."

"How did you get that, Annie?" Tommy asked.

"Patch broke off of his leash and ran into the garden and brought it back to me; it's my mum's."

"See, I told you, didn't I? People said funny goings-on in that house. I bet your mum is buried in the garden."

"Don't say nasty things like that, Tommy!"

Poor Annie started crying. Patch kept jumping up at her to console her. My god! What if Tommy was right; it doesn't bare thinking about.

"Hey, you two, don't forget about our plan for the weekend; what we said we would do at old Enid's cottage and that's only tomorrow now."

"Oh yes, and can I still come, Annie? Do you still like me?"

"Course I still like you, stupid."

47

"That's better and, Tommy, if you ask your parents if it's ok to stay over tonight, then we can all go off together in the morning."

"Oh great! Thanks, Dee."

"Right, make sure you come home together as I won't be able to meet you in time after school today."

"Bye, Dee."

"Bye."

When I got home, I phoned Val Smith and told her all about what happened this morning.

"Yes, Dee, I was about to call you. I have heard back from the police. Would you mind if we could come and see you this morning?"

"Yes, of course, I just want to get this all over and done with so we can get on with our lives."

"Hello again, Mrs King, DCI West here. We met at Miss Robertson's cottage last month."

"Oh yes, I remember. Do come in."

"And Val Smith, I believe you already know."

"Yes, please make yourself comfortable. I've just made a pot of tea."

"You know why we are here Mrs King? It's about Mrs Susan long and her mysterious disappearance."

"So what have you found out?"

"Well, we know that there is not any record of her death anywhere in the U.K., and after a lot of cross questioning with Mr long, he finally broke down and said his wife walked out on him and he doesn't know where she went to. Apparently, there is no relations to speak of."

"But why tell his daughter that she was dead?"

"He said he thought it would be kinder to Annie for her to think that as her mother didn't want her."

"I don't believe that for one minute. The way Annie talked about her mother, they adored one another. It was the father who didn't want her."

"Yes, he said about the way he has been with Annie and that was because she reminded him so much of his wife and he had to forget her."

"No, I'm sorry but that just doesn't warrant with me. I've also spoke with the man, and I like to believe I'm a good judge of people, and he is definitely no good."

"I do really sympathise with you, Mrs King, but people suffer in different ways, and I have no evidence on him without finding Mrs Long. We can only go on the truth at the moment that she has left him, and if I was her, I wouldn't want him to ever find me," he said laughingly.

"This morning, while you were there interviewing him, we walked past and our dog, Patch, slipped his lead and ran into the back garden of Mr Long."

"Yes, I saw you, Mrs King."

"But what you didn't see was what Patch had in his mouth and ran back to Annie with it."

"What was that, Mrs King?"

"A ribbon which I have here, and Annie said it was her mum's best ribbon, and she wore it all the time."

"Bit muddy, isn't it?"

"Yes, that's because Patch was digging in the garden and found it."

"Really? I would like to take this away to let forensics have a look at it."

"But Annie has asked me to put it somewhere safe in her room for when she gets home. She will be so upset."

"Look, I will work on it straight away and try my best to have it back before she gets home from school."

"Thank you so much, Mr West."

DCI West was true to his words and got back before Annie got home.

"What was that policeman doing here, Dee?"

"Oh, he just wanted to give me some papers from old Enid."

I hate telling fibs, but I just couldn't tell her the truth after all that she had been through. I just wanted her to be happy.

"Ok, you two, do you want to go upstairs to do your homework while I make tea?"

"Yes, Dee."

"I haven't got any, but I can help you, Annie."

"Come on then, yes and you, my lovely little Patch." Patch runs ahead.

'Ring, Ring'

"Hello, Mrs King, this is DCI West. I just wanted to say we have enough evidence to go and do a bit more searching at the Long household, and we are going in early in the morning, I just wanted to ask if you could keep Annie away from the area tomorrow. We don't want her walking in on us."

"No, of course not. We are out for the day tomorrow at Enid's cottage to do some clearing up, but thanks for letting me know."

After tea, we sat and watched a film on TV and spoilt ourselves with some sweets and a few treats for Patch. We couldn't leave him out now; he's also part of the family. What am I saying! Tommy isn't our family but he seems to be here more lately, but I wonder about his parents. I've never seen them, or heard from them. Surely, they are not up the pub every night. *Oh no, Dee, stop it, you have enough to worry about at the moment with Annie.*

That morning after breakfast, I made up a big pack lunch to take with us and drinks and then set off to Enid's cottage. Elizabeth had already phoned to say she would meet us there.

"Look, Dee, at how much ground there is here; it even goes down to a river."

"Yes, I just don't know where to begin, but we must make something of it so it will make Enid proud."

"Come on, let's go inside and do a bit of tidying up first."

"Here comes Elizabeth."

"Open the door for her would you, Tommy?"

"Hi, everyone, I've got hot drinks and sausage rolls on the way from the tea shop."

"Thanks, Liz, I'll just draw these curtains back then we can all sit down and have them."

As I went around drawing back the curtains and gradually letting the light in, I could feel the presence of old Enid around and imagining her sitting in her old rocking chair and pottering around the kitchen. Everything was dated; set back in the 50/60s era. I remember Dr Tindal saying that she had written a book; *that would be an interesting find.* It would give us a better insight on how she lived and thought.

Elizabeth and the kids were settled around the table with their hot drinks and sausage rolls so I also sat down and joined them.

"Now we have all got to think seriously what we are going to do here. What you kids said about having animals sounded a really good idea, and I thought of a name we could use to call it: *That's Patches Pet Home* – What do you all think?"

"Yes, Dee, that sounds great."

"The next thing is to see what land there is here, and what animals we are going to have and how we are going to run it?"

"We could have chickens," said Tommy.

"Rabbits," said Annie.

"A goat is a good idea to help keep all the grass down," said Elizabeth.

"There is so much to think of; we will have to build cages, fencing."

"We could also make it a school project. Anyone you know at school could come along and help out when they wanted to. You could put an advert on the school noticeboard, Tommy."

"Yes, that's a good idea, Dee. I will do that on Monday. Plus, we have the summer holidays coming up soon; that would give the kids round here something to do."

"And another thought; my grandkids are coming up next week. I could get them involved. Plus, if I get upstairs sorted out they could stay here for the weekend."

"A wonderful idea, Dee, but you know if you ever get stuck for space, you know I have that big old mansion where they could also stay."

"That's very nice of you, Elizabeth, thank you."

"Right why, don't you two go and have a good look around the garden and try and get some ideas, and I will go and sort out upstairs."

"And I will tidy up down here then, Dee."

We all got on with our jobs. I went upstairs and went into Enid's bedroom which gave me a bit of a cold feeling. How sad, this lady lived here all those years on her own; no family, just Patch to keep her company.

The first task was to pack away all her things. Luckily enough, we had thought of bags and boxes which the local shop had delivered there for us. Enid didn't have a lot of clothes but what was surprising – hanging there in the wardrobe – was her old nurses' uniform; all spic and span and covered in polythene. Perhaps we could also turn this cottage into a small museum and put Enid's uniform on display. There were a few pairs of shoes in the bottom of the wardrobe and a shoe box but no shoes in it. But very curiously, a few baby clothes, *how strange*. I was getting a bit stressed out. *These are someone's personal things. Who was I to chuck anything out. No, I will put everything in a box and they can all be stored in a spare room for now.* I went over to the dressing table; dusty glass trinkets trays and candle holders, a few little chains and a locket. I opened the locket. One side was a man who looked as if he was in a uniform and on the other side was a baby, all kinds of thoughts were going through my mind and then when I opened up a drawer I found the book that Dr Tindal had told me about. It was called, *My Life,* by Enid Robertson. Oh wow, how lovely! I could now read and get to know Enid much better and what she was like. I couldn't wait to get home and read it. But for now, I must get upstairs clean and tidy. "TEA UP," shouted out Elizabeth.

"Oh, Liz, You will never guess! I have found a book upstairs that Enid has written about her life. I can't wait to read it. When I've finished, you can also read it if you like."

"Oh yes! I would be very interested to."

Then the kids came running in, full of ideas for what they had seen outside in the gardens.

"Dee, you will have to get more animals. There is so much land. There is so much you can do. There's a kayak down by the water; you could also do rides."

"Calm down, Tommy. Stop getting over excited. We have plenty of time to sort things out."

"Dee, all the post I've found, I have put together in that box there some of them look like bills."

"Ok, Liz, I will take them back with me and go through them tonight."

That night after tea, Tommy stayed over again and they washed and dried up for me while I went through Enid's mail. After sorting out all the junk mail, there wasn't a lot left; an electric bill which wasn't much and a bank statement "My word!" I called out, "allowed £555.000 balance. What a lovely place we could create for Patch and Enid with that amount of money. I'd better send this through to Enid's solicitor tomorrow."

"Right, you two, I'm going to lay down and do some reading. Would you sort out a notice to put up at school on Monday?"

"Yes, Dee."
"Yes, Dee."

ENID'S BOOK

BORN IN 1925, I WAS THE ONLY CHILD, HAD A NORMAL UPBRINGING UNTIL THE WAR BEGAN. I WAS TRAINING AS A NURSE AND LIVED IN LONDON. ONE NIGHT WHILE I WAS AT WORK, I HEARD THAT THERE WAS AN AIR RAID OVER WHERE I LIVED. I PANICKED SO MUCH; WORRIED ABOUT MY PARENTS. SOON AS MY SHIFT FINISHED,

I RUSHED HOME ONLY TO FIND MY STREET WAS COMPLETELY DEMOLISHED; BRICKS AND RUBBLE EVERYWHERE, PEOPLE CRYING AND TRYING TO RESCUE PEOPLE THEY THOUGHT WERE STILL ALIVE. WHAT I THOUGHT WAS MY HOME, I TRIED TO WALK OVER THE RUBBLE, JUST TRYING TO FIND SOMETHING I COULD RECOGNISE FROM MY HOME. OH GOD! I PRAY THAT MY PARENTS MADE IT TO THE UNDER GROUND, SO TIRED AND WORRIED, I FELT I JUST WANTED TO COLLAPSE. THANK GOD FOR THE SALVATION ARMY, WHO WERE THERE MAKING TEA FOR EVERYONE AND HELPING WHERE THEY COULD. I DRAGGED MYSELF ALONG TO THE UNDERGROUND STATION. THERE WERE PEOPLE EVERYWHERE. A MAN AT THE ENTRANCE HAD A LONG LIST OF PEOPLE WHO HAD COME THROUGH, BUT MY PARENTS WERE NOT LISTED. I JUST SAT DOWN AND CRIED. I WAS ALL ALONE. NO ONE TO JUST GIVE ME A HUG AND HELP TAKE MY PAIN AWAY. AND THEN THIS SCRUFFY LITTLE DOG CAME UP TO ME AND PUT HIS PAWS ON ME, "HELLO, LITTLE MAN, HAVE YOU ALSO LOST YOUR LOVED ONES?" HE CUDDLED UP WITH ME. I NOTICED ON HIS COLLAR HIS NAME TAG HAD THE NAME OF PATCH ON IT. SOMEONE HANDED ME A BLANKET, AND PATCH AND MYSELF TRIED TO SNUGGLE DOWN AND KEEP WARM. THERE WERE MORE AIR RAIDS THAT NIGHT AND DUST WAS BLOWING IN DOWN THE TUNNELS.

THE NEXT DAY, I WENT OUT INTO THE DAYLIGHT. PATCH FOLLOWED ME BUT I HAD TO

GET BACK TO WORK AS I KNEW THEY WOULD NEED ME. AS I WALKED THROUGH THE MAIN DOORS, I LOOKED AT PATCH AND SAID TO HIM TO STAY AS I'VE GOT TO GO TO WORK AND HE WOULDN'T BE ALLOWED TO STAY WITH ME. AS I WALKED AWAY, HIS SAD LITTLE FACE, I WILL NEVER FORGET. HE JUST STOOD THERE LOOKING AT ME.

I WAS ALLOWED TO STAY AT THE NURSES' HOME DUE TO MY CIRCUMSTANCES AND THAT NIGHT AS I WALKED OUT OF THE HOSPITAL, WHO WAS THERE WAITING FOR ME? YES, MY NEW LITTLE FRIEND, PATCH.

"HELLO BOY! HAVE YOU BEEN WAITING FOR ME ALL DAY? YOU MUST BE HUNGRY AND THIRSTY. THERE IS A WATER TAP OVER HERE, COME AND GET A DRINK." PATCH LAPPED UP THE WATER FOR AGES. "YOU WERE A THIRSTY BOY. LET'S GO TO THE STORE AND SEE IF I CAN GET YOU A TIN OF FOOD AND THEN SOMEHOW, I AM GOING TO HAVE TO SNEAK YOU INTO MY ROOM AT THE NURSES' HOME." IT TURNED OUT THAT I WAS SHARING WITH ONLY ONE OTHER GIRL. "HELLO, MY NAME IS ENID."

"IT LOOKS LIKE I AM SHARING WITH YOU, AND MY NAME IS CAROL. PLEASE MAKE YOURSELF AT HOME, ENID, AND DON'T MIND ME, I AM ONLY HERE A COUPLE OF NIGHTS A WEEK. AND WHO IS THIS?"

"THIS IS PATCH. HE WILL NOT LEAVE ME. I FOUND HIM AT THE UNDERGROUND, OR RATHER HE FOUND ME THERE AND FOLLOWED ME TO THE

HOSPITAL THIS MORNING AND WAITED ALL DAY UNTIL I FINISHED WORK. HE MUST HAVE LOST HIS FAMILY LIKE ME."

"OH DEAR! THAT IS AWFUL. WELL, I WILL NOT SAY ANYTHING AS LONG AS HE IS QUIET. NO ONE SHOULD KNOW IF HE IS STAYING HERE."

"THANK YOU SO MUCH. HE HAS BEEN SO FAITHFUL AND COMFORTING FOR ME."

"NO WORRIES. THAT IS YOUR ROOM THERE IF YOU WANT TO UNPACK."

"OH, I DO NOT HAVE ANYTHING. IT WAS DESTROYED IN THE AIR RAID YESTERDAY. BUT I MANAGED TO GET ANOTHER UNIFORM FROM WORK AND THEY GAVE ME A SUB."

"WELL ANYTHING YOU WANT, JUST GO TO MY ROOM AND HELP YOURSELF."

"THANK YOU SO MUCH."

WELL CAROL WENT OUT AND SAID SHE WOULD NOT BE HOME TONIGHT. I FOUND A DISH AND FED PATCH THEN FOUND SOME CLEAN SHEETS AND MADE UP MY BED. I LOOKED IN CAROL'S ROOM TO SEE IF SHE HAD SOMETHING CASUAL I COULD WEAR, AND OH MY! THIS GIRL HAD SO MUCH CLOTHING AND SHE WAS THE SAME SIZE AS ME. WHAT LUCK! I FOUND A PAIR OF SLACKS AND A JUMPER, THEN HAD A BATH AND TOOK PATCH FOR A WALK. WE WALKED UP MY OLD STREET AGAIN. GUESS I WAS JUST HOPING TO SEE MY PARENTS TURN UP, BUT PEOPLE WERE STILL CLEARING THE AREA. THEN I HEARD SOMEONE CALL OUT "PATCH!

HERE, BOY!" PATCH WENT RUNNING UP TO THIS YOUNG MAN IN ARMY UNIFORM.

"IS HE YOUR DOG?"

"NO, HE BELONGED TO MY NEIGHBOUR, BUT UNFORTUNATELY THEY WERE KILLED YESTERDAY IN THE RAID AS ALSO MY PARENTS WERE."

"YES, I BELIEVE MY PARENTS WERE ALSO KILLED. OUR HOUSE WAS FLATTENED."

THE YOUNG MAN WAS VERY NICE AND CONCERNED. "SO DO YOU HAVE ANYWHERE TO STAY?"

"YES, I AM A NURSE, SO I AM STAYING THERE NOW. WHAT ABOUT YOU?"

"WELL, HALF MY HOME IS STILL INHABITABLE, SO AT LEAST I HAVE SOMEWHERE TO LAY MY HEAD WHILE I AM ON LEAVE, AND I CAN MAKE A CUP OF TEA ON THE STOVE WHICH IS STILL ALIGHT. PLEASE COME AND JOIN ME. I COULD REALLY DO WITH SOMEONE TO TALK TO. MY NAME IS BARRY, BY THE WAY."

"MINE IS ENID." I FELT THE SAME AND TOOK UP HIS OFFER OF TEA AND WE CHATTED INTO THE EARLY HOURS. I COULD NOT BELIEVE HOW FAST THE TIME FLEW.

"OH! AM I KEEPING YOU UP ENID?"

"NO, I HAVE A DAY OFF TOMORROW AND I AM ENJOYING OUR CHAT." BUT OUR CHAT WENT FURTHER AND I ENDED UP IN HIS BED. THIS WAS SOMETHING I HAD NEVER DONE BEFORE AND WAS SO OUT OF CHARACTER, BUT THEN THERE WAS

NOTHING NORMAL ABOUT WHAT WAS GOING ON IN THE WORLD TODAY. WE NEVER KNEW IF WE WOULD BE ALIVE THE NEXT DAY. YES, I ENJOYED MY NIGHT WITH BARRY. HE MADE LOVE TO ME SO GENTLY. I KNEW NOTHING ABOUT HIM, BUT I DID NOT CARE. IT WAS JUST NICE TO FORGET WHAT WAS HAPPENING AROUND US FOR A WHILE.

THE NEXT DAY, WE WALKED AND TALKED AND THEN THE BOMB SHELL. HE TOLD ME HE WAS GOING BACK TO WAR AGAIN TOMORROW.

"WILL I SEE YOU AGAIN, BARRY?"

"I HOPE SO, DEE, BUT WHILE THIS WAR IS ON. NO ONE CAN MAKE ANY PLANS, BUT PLEASE WRITE TO ME, ENID, AND I WILL WRITE TO YOU EVERY CHANCE I GET."

AND WE DID. I WROTE EVERY DAY AND I GOT ONE BACK FROM HIM EVERY WEEK. PATCH AND I GOT ON SO WELL. WHILE I WAS ON SHIFT, HE WOULD STAY IN THE BEDSIT AND STAY QUIET UNTIL I GOT HOME, THEN WE WOULD WALK AND PLAY WHEN I WAS HOME. SEVERAL WEEKS WENT BY AND I STARTED FEELING VERY TIRED AND SICK. I WENT TO SEE ONE OF OUR DOCTORS AT THE HOSPITAL ONLY TO FIND I WAS PREGNANT. I HAD SUCH MIXED FEELINGS. THIS WAS NOT THE RIGHT TIME TO BRING A BABY INTO THIS WORLD WITH ALL THAT WAS GOING ON, BUT AT THE SAME TIME, IT WAS THE CHILD OF THE MAN I LOVE. I WROTE A LOVELY LONG LETTER TO BARRY AND TOLD HIM ABOUT OUR BABY. WELL, I DO NOT KNOW IF HE GOT THAT LETTER BECAUSE TWO DAYS LATER I

GOT THE DREADED TELEGRAM FROM THE WAR DEPARTMENT, MY BARRY WAS DEAD (KILLED IN ACTION) MY WORLD HAD ONCE AGAIN FALLEN APART. PATCH KNEW SOMETHING WAS WRONG. HE SNUGGLED UP TO ME AND LICKED MY TEARS. THE MATRON TOOK ME TO ONE SIDE AND SAID IT WOULD RUIN MY LIFE NOW TO HAVE THIS BABY AND KEEP IT, AND THAT I WOULD NOT BE ABLE TO AFFORD TO LOOK AFTER IT AND SAID ABOUT ADOPTION. I SHRUGGED AT THAT THOUGHT, BUT SHE WENT ON TO SAY WHAT COULD YOU EVER GIVE THE CHILD AND IT COULD END UP BEING TAKEN AWAY FROM YOU FOR GOOD ANYWAY. I FELT LIKE I JUST WANTED TO DIE. MATRON SAID ABOUT THESE LOVELY PEOPLE SHE KNEW WHO COULD NOT HAVE CHILDREN AND THAT THEY WERE SO RICH THEY COULD GIVE MY BABY EVERYTHING. EVENTUALLY, I GAVE IN AND ARRANGED TO MEET THIS COUPLE TO SEE WHAT THEY WERE LIKE. THEY TURNED OUT TO BE VERY NICE AND PROMISED TO LOVE THE BABY AS THEIR OWN AND I BELIEVED THEM. THEY SEEMED VERY SINCERE.

THE DAY CAME WHEN I WENT INTO LABOUR. IT WAS HOURS. I THOUGHT TO MYSELF THIS BABY DOES NOT WANT TO COME INTO THIS WORLD, BUT THEN IT HAPPENED; MY BABY WAS BORN. IT WAS A LITTLE GIRL. SHE WAS BEAUTIFUL. HOW COULD I GIVE HER UP? SHE WAS SO HELPLESS. THE NEXT DAY, THE ADOPTED PARENTS TURNED UP TO TAKE HER AWAY I WAS NOT ALLOWED TO KNOW THERE

NAME OR ADDRESS BUT I ASKED THEM IF THEY WOULD TAKE THIS NOTE AND MY LOCKET WITH A PICTURE OF HER AND HER FATHER IN, AND WHEN THEY THOUGHT THE TIME WAS RIGHT IF THEY WOULD GIVE IT TO HER AND THEY AGREED, YES THEY WOULD. A YEAR OR MORE PAST BY AND I GOT A LETTER FROM THE LOCAL COUNCIL THAT THEY HAD SORTED OUT ALL THE BOMB DAMAGE DONE IN THE ROAD WHERE I HAD LIVED AND I WAS OWED MONEY FOR THAT.

"HEY, PATCH, WE HAVE COME INTO SOME MONEY, AND YOU AND I ARE GOING TO MOVE TO THE COUNTRY WHERE I KNOW MY LITTLE GIRL IS LIVING, WHICH BROUGHT US TO BURGH ST PAUL. AS THAT WAS ALL I KNEW ABOUT WHERE MY LITTLE GIRL HAD GONE."

AND WE FOUND THIS LOVELY LITTLE COTTAGE. I GOT PATCH A GIRLFRIEND SO HE WAS NOT LONELY WHEN I WAS AT WORK. HER NAME WAS LIZZIE. THEY WERE HAPPY AND HAD PUPPIES.

Oh no! I can't read any more of this. My god! This lady Enid is Elizabeth's mother. I looked at my watch at the time; it was nine pm. I must phone Liz.

"Liz, it's Dee. I have something very urgent to speak to you about. Can you get over? I would come to you but the kids are in bed now."

"Yes, of course, Dee. I will drive over. Will be there in tem minutes."

"Hi, what's up. Dee?"

"Oh Lizzie! I think I have found your mother."

"What, what are you saying? How?"

"I've just been reading Enid's book. Look, I will go and make a cup of tea, although I think we might need something stronger, and you start reading that." And handed her the book.

Liz started reading the book. I made a cup of tea and quietly put it down beside her. I could see by the expression on her face that she was really getting into it. After an hour or so, she gradually looked up at me and said, "Can it be true, Dee?"

"Well, it's such a coincidence, don't you think?"

"But she is now dead. I can't even get a DNA done."

"She might be dead, but she is not buried yet."

"What?"

"No, there has been quiet a back-log apparently. They couldn't sort her burial out for a month, and it's next Wednesday."

"Oh, Dee. I'm shaking so much. What do I do now? I can't think."

"Just try and relax. Here, have a glass of wine and I will go and phone Dr Tindal."

"Dr Tindal, I'm sorry to call you so late, but this is Dee King and I've got Elizabeth Browne here, and we have been reading old Enid's book and it looks like Lizzie is her long-lost daughter from the war and Enid's being buried next Wednesday. Can Liz still get a DNA done in time?"

"Hang on there, I will be over in a jiffy," he said and put the phone down.

"Liz, Dr Tindal is coming straight over."

"Thank you for coming over, doctor. I'm so sorry to have called you out so late."

"No worries, my dear. I'm a bit of a knight owl. Besides, what you have told me about old Enid. Well this has to be sorted out very quickly. You know she is being buried on Wednesday?"

"Yes, I know. Please come through and I will make us a hot drink."

"Hello, Mrs Browne."

"Oh please, call me Elizabeth or Lizzie. This is so good of you to come."

"I am just as keen on finding out also, my dear, especially when families are involved. I just need to take a couple of test, then I will take them to the hospital lab myself tomorrow and hopefully we will know by Monday. Funny, old Enid was so secretive about her past, and I've known her for some years now. She was a good nurse, and I know she moved here from London with her dog, Patch. Obviously not the same Patch that young Annie has now, but every dog she had, she called him Patch, but mind you, they all came from the same family. She got a female friend for Patch and they had pups and she always kept one of each sex until they also had pups, but the eldest boy she would call Patch. I asked her why, and she said this dog called Patch came to her rescue during an air raid on London. He also lost his owners as Enid lost her parents, and he never left her side, so it was like Patch never died, as there was always one of his pact to carry on. She loved them all so very much."

"That's such a lovely story. I'm so glad we found her book, otherwise we would never have known."

"I would love to read it, ladies, when you have finished."

"Yes of course, doctor, no problem."

"Well that's me, done. I will get off now and let you know the results ASAP."

"Goodnight, doctor, and thanks once again."

"Lizzie, it is so late now, why don't you stay here the night?"

"Do you know, Dee, I don't think I can be on my own anyway tonight. Thank you, I will stay."

I went and got some clean sheets and a quilt from the airing cupboard and made up a bed in the lunge for Elizabeth, then Patch came quietly down the stairs and went up to Elizabeth, knelt down and put his paws on her lap, just as the old Patch did to Enid in the underground. How strange! Do they really have a sixth sense like people say? If that is so then what about all his behaviour with Annie's father and digging in his garden. Oh no! I completely forgot about the police going round to Annie's old house and investigating more. I wonder how they got on?

"Bed's all made, Lizzie. Please help yourself to anything you need. I'm off to bed myself now."

"Thank you, Dee. Please keep this just between us for now until we know the truth."

"Yes of course I will; night."

"Tommy, wake up."

"Oh, what? I'm still tired."

"Lizzie is asleep downstairs on the sofa."

"So what?"

"Well she wasn't here last night when we went to bed."

"Yes, I did hear some talking downstairs before I dropped off to sleep. I must say this bed is so comfy I don't want to get up."

"Morning, you two. Ready for some breakfast?"

"Yes please, Dee. Dee, why is Lizzie sleeping downstairs?"

"She came to help me with some paperwork last night and it got late so I made her a bed up."

"Are we going back to the cottage today, Dee?"

"Yes, if you want to there is plenty to do there, and so much to sort out."

'Ring Ring.'

"Oh! Hello, inspector."

"Mrs King, would it be possible to come along and see you tomorrow? Annie will be at school, won't she?"

"Yes, around ten. Of course I'll be here."

"What did he want, Dee?"

"Nothing, just a chat."

We got to Enid's cottage around eleven that morning and decided to have a stroll around the gardens. The children were right; there was a lot of ground here and so many passages to walk along. One of them brought us up to the old church at the far end of the cemetery and straight away, Patch ran off the same corner as before and started digging.

"Patch, come here! Stop that digging."

"Patch, no! You will have the reverend after us come away."

With reluctance, Patch came back to Annie and we carried on down another passage which led us to the river. The sun shone across the water. It looked beautiful and calm. There was a pontoon with an old dingy tied to it. This time, Patch decided to run in the water and have a swim.

"We should all bring our swimming costumes next time and go swimming," Annie said.

"Yes, it looks nice and inviting, doesn't it?"

"Let's try out the dingy," Tommy said.

"We don't know who it belongs to. We had better not, but we can put that on our list of things to do. Get a new dingy or kayak, and do you know what else, I thought of walking around here; there is so much ground to cover, why don't we invest in a train?"

"A TRAIN?"

"Not a big one, a small engine like you see in pleasure parks with a little carriage and a track going all around the grounds."

"Yes, that sounds fun, Dee."

"Well, I've got news for you guys. Up in one of the garages at the mansion is an old steam train with carriage. I'm sure it won't take much to get it going again."

"Lizzie, that's terrific."

"What I think we ought to do when we are ready to go full ahead into this venture, we must take on a full time handyman and gardener and they could live in the cottage."

"Yes, good idea, Dee. I wish I was old enough to do it." Tommy said.

"Well, you never know, Tommy. When you leave school, you might be running this place."

"Yes and I can run a riding school," said Annie.

"I can see a lot of potential coming to this place thanks to Enid."

"Oh look! I just saw a deer running through the woods."

"There must be lots of animals around here running wild. We shall have to take care of them and make sure they have a nice environment always."

The grounds just went on and on. There was a little pond and still had fish in it and a frog, water lilies, rockeries, and flowers. It was so pretty and then a long cobbled pathway leading to a little outhouse or maybe a sun-house. We walked in and it looked like at one time someone lived there. There was a lounge area with a galley style kitchenette and through the back door to a bedroom and bathroom, small but very compatible, outside was various outbuildings. There was so much scope here, but I could tell it was going to be a full time job and we were going to need help.

"Well, I don't know about you, Liz, but so much has been going through my mind and ideas."

"Yes, I'm sorry, Dee. I've been so quiet. It's just all day I have been thinking, of you know what? I'm finding hard to concentrate."

"I know, Liz. Me too. Say I've got a nice big joint slowly cooking in the oven, come back with us and have Sunday dinner."

"Haven't I inconvenienced you enough, Dee?"

"No. We are friends and always will be, I hope."

"Yes, we sure are, Dee, and yes I would love dinner."

"What about you, Tommy? Will you be allowed to come back for dinner?"

"Oh yes, please."

"But you must ask your parents."

"No, they won't mind really."

"Do you know, Lizzie, it really worries me about young Tommy."

"Why what do you mean, Dee?"

"Well, I love having him come round, and he and Annie are such good friends, but I have never seen his parents. I just take his word that everything is alright with them, and that he is allowed to stay whenever he wants. He told me once that they never get back till after closing time at the pub. I just don't know what to think. I just know it would make me feel a lot better if I could see them."

"Yes, I must admit, Dee, that does sound a bit strange. But I'm sure you are worrying a bit too much about it. Besides, don't you think you have enough to worry about right now?"

"Yes, you're right, and that reminds me, I've got that policeman coming tomorrow, which reminds me, would you do me a big favour and walk Tommy home after dinner, as I have to keep Annie away from her old house, for now?"

"Yes, Dee, I will."

We all sat down to a nice Sunday roast, which everyone enjoyed and we had jelly and ice cream afterward and Patch enjoyed his Sunday treat also.

"Oh, Tommy my love, Lizzie is going to walk back home with you tonight, is that alright?"

"You don't have to, really, I'm ok walking on my own. I've done a lot of it."

"Yes, I know, Tommy, but it would put my mind at rest knowing your home safely."

That evening, Annie and I had some me time together, played an old game of snakes and ladders, which Annie had never played before and really enjoyed it.

Monday came around and Annie went off to school, and I got on with my Monday morning chores.

'Knock Knock.'

"Hello, Mr West. Do come in and sit down. The kettle has just boiled."

"Well, Mrs King, things are looking a bit suspicious at the Longs' home. We have had to start digging up the garden, unfortunately, because we have found a lot of women's clothing buried there, and Mr Long's excuse is that he buried it after she had left because he didn't want Annie to see anything left there. But I don't believe a word the man says, so we are digging more."

"Oh no! So do you think he has killed her?"

"We are not ruling that out, Mrs King."

'Ring Ring.'

"Hello, Yes he's here. It's for you, Mr West."

"Hello, Ok, I'll be right over."

"Well, Mrs King, it looks like we will soon have the mystery sorted. They have found a body and it's a live one; being held captive in a cellar beneath the house, and we believe it to be Mrs Long."

"I don't know what to say. How awful! Do you need me to come with you, Mr West?"

"That might be a good idea, Mrs King. We don't know what sort of state she will be in, and perhaps another woman there might help. They have called the local doctor to come and see her also, and Mr Long has been arrested and taken away."

When we got to the Longs' house, there were several police cars outside. Dr Tindal was already there trying to examine Mrs Long, who looked dreadful with black greasy tatty hair. What clothes she did have on were ripped to shreds, she was covered in cuts and bruises and she just sat there staring into space and not saying a word. Dr Tindal said she was so traumatised and badly beaten that she was suffering from shock, and it would take some time before she would come round properly and be able to talk.

"Dr Tindal, could I just speak to Mrs Long just for one moment?"

"Yes, my dear, But I don't think you will get any reaction from her yet."

I knelt down in front of Mrs Long and held her hand, but she didn't move an inch.

"Mrs Long, you don't know me, but my name is Dee, and for the last few weeks now, I have been looking after a lovely young girl called Annie."

With that, her eyes turned and stared at me. It was a bit frightening.

"Yes, Annie, your daughter who loves you so much and thought you were dead." Her hand then grabbed mine and the woman had a tear in her eye.

"Yes, she loves you and misses you so much and can't wait to see you again, and I will carry on looking after her till you are better again, so don't you worry; just hurry up and get better again and when the time is right, I will tell her you are still very much alive and can't wait to see her again."

"That's good advice, Mrs King, not to tell young Annie yet. Let her mother get back on her feet first."

"Yes, I agree with that," said Dr Tindal.

"I had better get off. Annie will be home soon. What will happen now with Mrs Long?"

"She is going into hospital to be examined and then take it from there, Mrs King. Can I call round this evening and could you ask your friend, Elizabeth, to be there also?"

"Yes sure, would seven be alright?"

"Yes, see you both then."

I went off to meet Annie from school. As usual, Tommy would be walking beside her, coming out of the school grounds. I kept thinking about that poor woman and what she must have been going through and how I was going to have to keep it from Annie, but at the same time, how was I going to tell her she was still alive.

"Let's go and get an ice cream, you two."

"Perhaps we could have an ice cream stall at our zoo when it's finished."

"Oh, it's a zoo now?" I said laughing.

"Well, it's big enough, Dee."

"There are lots of things we can do there, but it will take a bit of time."

"Why isn't Patch with you, Dee?"

"Oh, I had to leave him at home today as I had to go and talk to DCI West about something."

"Was it about my dad, Dee?"

"Yes, Annie it was, because they didn't believe that your mum had passed away last year, and after a long talk to your father, he is now saying that your mum left him and that it was easier to tell you that she was dead."

"No no, my mum would never have left me behind, Dee. He has killed her, I know he has."

"No he hasn't, my love. That's what the police thought, but they have found her!"

"What!"

"Yes, she is not very well, and she is getting good care now and soon as she is better you can see her."

Annie broke down crying. Tommy put his arm around her. I held her hand across the table. I just had to tell her. I couldn't keep it in any longer; letting her think her mother was dead when she wasn't.

"I love my mother, Dee, but I couldn't go back and live the way we did with my father there."

"That won't happen, Annie. When your mum is better, it will just be you and her."

"And me, Annie." Tommy said.

"We will all still be together, my lovelies, just be patient a little longer. Mr West and Dr Tindal are keeping me informed. In fact, Dr Tindal is coming round tonight to see Lizzie as he may have some good news for her."

"What's that, Dee?"

"Well Lizzie never knew her real mum, and reading through old Enid's book, it looks like she could be Lizzie's mum."

"Really? Oh Dee! Can I come round tonight? I love hearing people get good news."

"But if Lizzie turns out to be Enid's daughter, that means we lose our zoo."

"I shouldn't worry about that. Lizzie is just as excited as we are so I'm sure she will carry on with it."

'Knock Knock.'

"Come in, Dr Tindal. Lizzie is in the lounge."

"Well, Lizzie, I can see you have your fan club with you."

Woff woff!

"Yes and Patch."

"I've got your results here. I haven't opened it yet as you can see, so I'm just as in the dark as you, so here goes."

Dr Tindal was quiet for what seemed to be such a long time, but probably only seconds, then he looked up. With a serious face, he looked at every one of us and then looked back to Lizzie. Oh dear! It doesn't look like good news. Then he spoke in a solemn way.

"Mrs Elizabeth Browne, I have to inform you from the DNA test taken from you and matched up with Miss Enid Robertson that the test shows... YOU ARE THE DAUGHTER OF ENID."

Everyone jumped for joy. I opened a bottle of champagne, which I had put by ready and hoping that the news was good. Lizzie broke down crying. I handed her and Dr Tindal a glass of champagne.

"I finally found my real mum and now she is dead, if only I could have spoken to her."

"My dear, she is just down the road in the chapel of rest as she is not being buried till Wednesday. Why don't you go and see her?"

"Yes, I can come with you, Lizzie, for moral support."

"Yes please, Dee, I would like that. Where is she being buried, Dr Tindal?"

"In her own grounds, my dear. That's why it took so long to arrange, and the ceremony is at St Mary's church."

That next day, I went with Lizzie to the chapel of rest. I waited outside while Lizzie went through to see her mother.

The funeral director pulled back the cloth covering Enid. She looked beautiful and at peace; all the pain had gone from her. In her hands was a locket open, showing the pictures of her lover and her baby, and in the other hand was an old dog collar which had belonged to her first dog, Patch.

"Oh mum! I so wished we met and talked, You did give me to a wonderful family, and they gave me so much love and I never wanted for nothing. I like that you became a nurse but I looked after animals, not people. I got married and we both became vets and got our own practice in London. We had a daughter, Susan, but she grew up and got mixed up with this very awful man. She wouldn't listen to us and would not have a word said against him. She ran away with him in the end, and I've not seen her since. That was fifteen years ago now, and she is in her thirties. I think she must have changed her name because I cannot find her, and her father died a few years ago. My adopted parents died a short while ago in a car accident, so I had no one left, and now I am back here in burgh St Paul living in the big red house mansion, and little did I know you were just down the road from me. I did go to St Mary's church and I met a lovely lady there called Dee, and now we are best of friends and I am going to make you proud, mum, with your lovely cottage and grounds. It will all be dedicated to you and Patch. We have some wonderful ideas and you will be proud. Rest well, my dear mother, and we will meet again."

Lizzie came out of the side room in tears.

"Come on, Lizzie, let's go and get a coffee."

"Will you come to the funeral with me tomorrow, Dee?"

"Yes of course, and the kids and not to forget Patch."

That evening, I got a phone call from DCI West saying that all being well, Annie might be able to see her mum on Friday, which made Annie happy as it gave her a piece of mind about when she was going to see her mum again.

"Dee! I have made some quick arrangements for the funeral tomorrow. I thought it would be nice to do a small spread of food at the cottage after the ceremony, so I have arranged for caterers to come in. I know we could have done it ourselves, but there really isn't much time to do shopping etc., and I wanted us to all relax and enjoy our last day with Enid and who ever turns up at the funeral."

"That's a lovely gesture, Elizabeth, and you are right; so much has happened in these last couple of days, you finding your mother and Annie finding out that her mother is still alive. It's like a fairy tale."

FUNERAL DAY

Michael greeted us at the door of the church.

"Hello, ladies. Old Enid should be arriving soon by a horse-drawn carriage and the pull bearers have been arranged, and I guess, Elizabeth, you would want to follow behind your mother down the aisle?"

"Yes, father, and I would like my new found friends here to join me."

"But of course, my dear, and the seating right at the front has been made available for all of you."

Enid's carriage pulled up and it looked so beautiful, Elizabeth had arranged with the florist to spare no expense on the flowers, and they worked all through the night to get them done. One side of the coffin said mother and the other side said grandmother. I keep forgetting Elizabeth has a daughter.

We followed behind the coffin down the aisle. A song was playing, *lord hear my prayer.* There were quite a few people who had attended. Michael Heart, the reverend, gave a beautiful speech and also brought Elizabeth into it, the long lost daughter, and of course Patch. When the ceremony was over, Enid's coffin was carried outside and along a path into Enid's property, and there in a plot of its own, where Enid was to be buried, stood a big monument of her first dog, Patch, who comforted her during the war when she lost her parents. Elizabeth invited the people who attended the funeral into the cottage for a gathering afterwards, which was nice for her as she could hear more stories about the mother she never knew. Even the reverend, Michael, knew Enid very well and said she never missed Sunday service and there was a day every week she would go there just to be alone and pray. He believed it was a Wednesday.

"Dee! Elizabeth! Come quick, Patch started digging again in that corner of the church yard and there is something there."

Liz and I quickly got up to go and see what it was they had found. It was the same spot every time; just in the corner of the church grounds before you enter into Enid's land. Patch obviously knew something was there. As we got closer, we could see earth everywhere that he had dug up. What a mess! Patch was standing over the hole he had dug, panting very heavily. Looking down the hole, we could just make out some kind of bundle wrapped in material a curtain perhaps. Liz knelt down and reached out to touch the bundle. I could see the look of shock in her eyes.

"Right, kids, come away from here now and inside."

"What is it, Liz?"

"It's an animal of some kind. So I need to get the reverend."

"Oh I wondered what you were going to say, Liz, going by the look on your face."

"I just wanted to get the kids out of the way, Dee. It's not an animal. It's the skull of a baby."

"You're kidding me, no? What more can happen in this village?"

"Let's get back indoors and talk to the reverend, and we had better call the police."

"Michael! Did you know there was a baby buried on the church grounds in an unmarked grave?"

"What!"

"Yes, Patch has just dug it up."

"Are you sure? We must call the police. Ladies, please excuse me. I must get back to the rectory and sort this out."

"Yes, father, let us know if there is anything we can do to help."

"Thank you, must go now."

"Don't you think we should go with him also, Liz?"

"No, Dee, it's on his ground, and we have enough on our plate to deal with at the moment."

"Yes, you're right. Next move is to take Annie to see her mum on Friday."

'Ring Ring.'

"Hello."

"Hello, Mrs King, it's DCI West speaking. Sorry to have to bother you again, but I just wanted to clarify if it was you who found the remains of a baby at the church yard yesterday?"

"Well, not exactly. We were all there: Liz, myself, Annie and Tommy, and of course Patch, who dug it up. But it was Liz who put her had down the hole and discovered it. But we told the children it was an animal so not to upset them."

"Oh I see. Well, from what we can tell at the moment is that the baby could have been still born and the mother tried to get rid of it. But it going to take some time before we can find out exactly what happened, that's if we ever can find out. It looks like the baby had been buried there six to twelve months, but somewhere out there is a mother that knows who it is. I must say, Mrs King, that dog of yours would be a big help to us at the station. First he uncovers Mrs Longs' clothing in the garden and now this baby. Yes, he would make a good police dog."

"Well, I don't know about that Mr West. He is too attached to Annie now."

"Yes I know, but perhaps she would let us borrow him sometime if we need to dig up anything?"

"I'm sure she would Mr. West. Is it still alright to visit Annie's mother tomorrow?"

"Yes. It's all arranged for 4 pm, but tell her not to expect a lot out of her at the moment. She has been very traumatised, and it will take time. But she looks a lot better than when we found her. Well, I will say goodbye for now and hope all goes well tomorrow."

"Yes. Goodbye, Mr West."

I met Annie from school that day and took her to visit her mum. A nurse showed us into this room where Mrs Long was sitting in a corner just staring out of the window.

"Mum! Oh mum!"

Mrs Long slowly turned her head to face Annie and managed a little smile, then turned her head back to look out of the window.

"Doesn't she recognise me, Dee?"

"Annie, all you can do at the moment is give her time. She has been very ill and it will take time for her to get back to normal again. But we can help by keep coming to see her and reassuring her and most of all loving her."

Annie went up to her mother and sat down beside her and held her hand.

"Oh, mum, I thought you were dead. Dad told me you were dead, and dad said he wished I died with you, and told me to clear off, and I slept in a church all week and this lovely lady here, mum, she found me and looked after me and still is. Then a dog called Patch found me also, as his owner died and chose to come and stay with me and we love each other to bits. It was him that found you. In fact, he is so clever, he found a buried animal in the church yard. We thought it was a baby."

With that Annie's mum quickly turned her head round and grabbed Annie's hand so hard.

"Oh, Annie, I think you have filled your mum's brain with so much so fast. She can't keep up with you. Slow down just a little bit."

"I'm sorry. I've got so much to tell her, but she must know me, Dee. Did you see the way she squeezed my hand then?"

"Yes, I did, my love, of course she knows who you are."

At that moment, a doctor came in and introduced himself to us and asked if we were related to Ann.

"This is Susan's daughter Annie, and I am a friend looking after her. My name is Dee."

"Dee, could we leave Annie with her mother for a few minutes while we have a chat outside?"

"Yes, doctor. Annie, I will just be outside if you need me."

"Ok, Dee."

I followed the Doctor outside into the corridor.

"Well, Dee, I don't know how long it's going to be before Susan is back to nothing again. I have never seen such abuse in my life as I have with this woman. She has been beaten continually for how long, I don't know. She has been starved. In fact, she would have been dead very shortly if she hadn't been found in time, and now we have just discovered that she has had an abortion within the last year."

"Oh doctor! Please call DCI West at the police station. We found an unborn child buried at the church yard last Wednesday."

"Well, that is a coincidence! That was my next job, to phone the police. I will get on to it now."

I went back into the side ward with Annie and her mum. Annie was still chatting away to her mum, but this time, mum had turned around with her head down holding Annie's hand.

"Dee, mummy said she loved me."

"That's good, Annie. See! She is slowly making progress. Do you think we should let her rest now and come and see her again tomorrow?"

"Yes, Dee. We should let her rest. Mum, we are going now, but we will be back tomorrow, alright?"

She squeezed her hand again and Annie gave her a big hug and a kiss goodbye.

"Goodbye, Mrs Long. Great to see you again, and you look a lot better than the first time we met. Will see you also tomorrow."

She looked up at me with tears in her eyes.

When we got home, Tommy was waiting outside with Patch. We all went indoors and I got some tea on the go. I gave Liz a call. I just had to tell her about the baby and

Annie's mum, who was astounded as much as I was. It was a good thing the kids were on summer holidays next week for six weeks. We had so much to do and get on with. That evening, there was a knock on the door; it was Liz.

"Dee, DCI West phoned me and asked me to come here and meet him and Dr Tindal, but didn't say why; just that it was important."

"Well, you better come in. I wonder what it's all about?" At 7 pm, there was a knock on the door.

"Yes, come in, Mr West and Dr Tindal. I must say this is a surprise."

"Ladies, please be seated. Now, do the children know about the baby we found?"

"So it was a baby we found. Tommy said it was, but you told us it was an animal."

"That's because of everything that has happened lately, we didn't want to give you more to worry about."

"Well anyway, Dr Tindal here after doing the DNA for you, Elizabeth, he got more interest in it and he has found that he could also get a DNA from the dead baby."

"Really, do you have to do that now, doctor. I think we know who the baby is."

"Well, Dee, it gets more complicated than that. You see, it also matches up with old Enid." The room went quite; you could hear a pin drop.

"So that means it must match me."

"Yes, that's right, Elizabeth. It does."

"But I thought the baby belonged to Annie's mother?"

"Yes it does, Elizabeth."

"Ok what's going on? I don't understand you grownups."

"Annie, what is your mother's name?"

"Susan Long."

"Are you going to see her again tomorrow?"

"Yes, why?"

"I would like to come with you, Annie, because I think your mum might be my daughter who I haven't seen in years."

With that, Patch jumped up with joy, wagging his tail and barking.

"That dog knows. He has found all of us and got us back together."

"I told you that dog was clever."

Everyone now was chatting. If this all turns out to be true, which it looks like it does, I'm soon going to be on my own again. I'm not going to be wanted after this. Annie will have her mother back and now she has a grandmother and a great grandmother who owns all that land, let alone all the ground and property Elizabeth has. Yes, it will be back to a little old lady in her cottage on her own again. But I must say, it was nice while it lasted. Patch must have known how I was feeling; he came over to me, sat down and put his paw on my lap.

"You're a good boy, Patch. You have made a lot of people happy."

"Hey, Dee, don't forget you also are part of our family."

"Bless you, Annie. I hope you will always keep in touch."

"What are you talking about, Dee? Don't forget our enterprise we are starting up. You can't back out now; you're a part of it."

"Thank you, Lizzie, I'm looking forward to it."

"And what about me? Yes, you forgot about me. I'm not related," says Tommy.

"Oh yes you are, Tommy. You promised me when we get older you were going to marry me. I hope you haven't gone back on your word." says Annie

"Right. We will get engaged and make it official."

We all laughed.

Elizabeth and Annie went to the hospital.

"Oh my god! Susan, you are my daughter."

Susan turned around and looked at Elizabeth and screamed out "Mum!"

Susan broke down crying and hugged her mum and her daughter. She had got her memory back. It was so wonderful to see nan, mum and daughter all reunited again and so happy.

"Dee, I'm going to take my daughter back home with me. We have a lot of catching up to do. And now knowing little Annie is my granddaughter, I have a lot of sorting out to do. You have taken Annie into your home and cared for her so much. Please, Dee, can she still stay with you a little while longer, so that I can get my daughter on her feet again and to find out what has gone on in her life with that pig she was with. I don't know how they are going to feel, but I would like to turn part of the mansion into a home just for them so that they can live independently on their own with no bother from me; only when they want to of course. And, Dee, that got me thinking I could also do the same for you. Why don't you sell up here put your money away and come and live with us also? Please don't say anything now; think about it. I have such a big place up there. I could convert it into three or four flats easily. We would all have our own privacy and the main hall could be a meeting point if we wanted to get together. So much has happened, Dee, and it's all because of you. If you hadn't found Annie that day in the church, if you hadn't met me that day in the church, who knows what would have happened."

"Lizzie, thank you so much. You and Annie and Tommy have bought so much joy and happiness into my life. I don't know where I would be without you now."

Well, time went on and a day didn't go past without anything to do. Lizzie got the architects working on the plans for conversion to the mansion while getting to know her daughter again, and Annie, Tommy and myself worked on Enid's cottage. We got a handyman to come and live in. He chose to live in the garden ranch at the bottom of the property as there were lots of out buildings for him to work in. My grandchildren also came up in the holidays to help out. They all had their own interest, which they got on with. Max was in charge of the boats down on the water edge, Toby was in charge of the train and making carriages, Tommy was in charge of laying the track, Sam was in charge of the bunnies and feeding them, Annie was in charge of the birds, putting up feeding tables and feed and water tables, and then my eldest granddaughter, Sophie, when she wasn't working, would come along and help out everyone with advice if they needed it. And myself, well I kept them all fed and watered. Our handyman, Bill, was a great help landscaping the grounds when the kids weren't getting in his way. But he didn't mind. He liked kids and had a joke with them.

So we were beginning to be a big success. We had a meeting and decided to call our project ENID'S PATCH, ANIMAL PARK.

My daughter in law, Tiffany, suggested we got horses, which gave me another idea. My son, Gary, was a fully trained mechanic and we didn't have a garage local and had to drive fifteen miles away, so I said to them why don't they think of selling up moving into my cottage or this cottage and Gary could also have his own garage on the grounds and Tiffany could run the riding stables. The school is near for the boys, and we could all work together. I said to think on it, there's enough ground here to do what they want.

Christmas was here and it was cold and the snow laid on the ground. We were all going to spend it together at the big house.

The main hall looked so festive. A table filled the middle of the room enough for about forty people and laid out with everyone's name at their place. Elizabeth had invited everyone, even Mrs Adams from the post office, DCI West, the reverend, Dr Tindal, not forgetting old Bill, the handyman, and all my family. Tommy, Patch, Annie and everyone who cared and mattered were there, and it was beautiful and a massive twenty-foot Christmas tree with masses of presents all around.

"Dee, come with me. I've got something to show you."

Elizabeth took me to the west wing of the mansion and handed me a key.

"Merry Christmas, Dee. Your suite is all ready for you."

I was gobsmacked. I had no idea this was anywhere near finished yet. I unlocked the massive door, which opened to a large hallway with so many doors off of it, and stairs which went up one side and come down the other a big chandelier in the centre, which I jokingly said I will never be able to clean! I walked up and around the stairs which had double doors, opening to the master bedroom. The Ritz had nothing on this, a massive whirlpool bath, a shower cubicle you could get six people in, the other side of the room was a walk-in wardrobe.

When I was younger, I could have filled it with all my clothes but not now. Then in the middle of the room were double patio doors which opened onto a gorgeous terrace with table and chairs lounger and shrubs and overlooked the outdoor swimming pool. We walked back down the stairs to see what was there; there were bedroom after bedroom, a study, a games room, a TV room, and the kitchen was something to die for! There was a range, a fridge, drinks fridge, another massive table which seated about twelve, dishwashers, double sink and drainers, double doors onto the patio and swimming pool. Then Liz said, "Just one more room, Dee."

"But, Liz, this is too big for me," I said, and as she opened the door and said as a crowd roared,

"No, this isn't. You're one, Dee. It's for your kids." I nearly fainted. There was Gary and Tiffany and boys and behind them were a crowd of friends all cheering and clapping. So my son, daughter-in-law and grandkids were moving in; I was so happy.

"And, Dee, you are over the other side; same design, but a bit smaller for you, just like mine in the other corner. And to the front of mine is for my daughter and granddaughter, and that's the real key for you, Dee. I hope you will all be happy. Oh and by the way! In the middle of the mansion is a gym and steam room and indoor swimming pool."

"Lizzie, I don't know what to say. I am lost for words. This is like a fairy tale. How can I ever repay you?"

"You don't. I have more money than I could ever spend. Thanks to Enid leaving me with the richest people around when I was born and the uncanny thing is, this property has a walkway through to Enid's land, so I think we can make Enid's Patch even bigger."

Enid's Patch was opened the following year. It was fantastic and everyone helped and was happy. We had a train that took you around the grounds boat by the river, no end of bird boxes everywhere, horses, lamas, chickens, tortoise, bunnies, squirrels, pheasants and a peacock.

Tiffany was busy with the horses and giving riding lessons, and Gary had built his garage next to the car park to the grounds and in no time things were really looking up. I even found out the mystery of young Tommy. He also didn't have any parents and was being brought up by his older brother, Ken, who told him not to tell anyone or they would take him away. So now, Tommy lives with me and helps Gary out at weekends in the garage as he wants to be a mechanic and save lots of money so he can marry Annie.

THE END

(OR IS IT?)